A TASTE LIKE SIN

PAINTED SIN BOOK 2

LANA SKY

A Taste like Sin

A Taste like Sin By Lana Sky

This is a work of fiction. Names, characters, businesses, places, events and incidents are either the products of the author's imagination or used in a fictitious manner. Any resemblance to actual persons, living or dead, or actual events is purely coincidental.

Cover Design by Charity Chimni
Editing by Mickey Reed Editing
Formatting by Charity Chimni
Proofreading by Charity Chimni

ONE

Real monsters hide their true identities behind their polished masks. But broken little girls? We disguise our pain with rebellion.

For instance, when faced with her father's betrayal, in what ways might a sheltered socialite lash out? Why, by selling her virginity to none other than said father's sworn enemy.

And where might such a man take her in order to culminate her pain and humiliation?

To view an orgy, of course. In all fairness, I all but dared him to.

Distract me was the challenge I proposed to Damien Villa after spending forty-eight hours locked inside my apartment. It's only fitting that he picked his favorite arena to amuse me within—as well as to reinforce the bargain we've struck: I've sold my virginity to him for a dangerous price. *His* company.

"You're shaking, Ms. Thorne," Damien acknowledges, his coarse tone like velvet against my eardrum. He's seated on a leather chair beside the identical one I'm perched on the edge of. Only a sliver of space separates us and, this close, his heat is a cruel, mocking taste of what I can't seem to feel: anything.

The aftermath of Heyworth's deception has rendered me hollow.

Empty.

Numb.

Though my nails dig into my palms—I'm clenching them that tightly—nothing cuts through the fog in my brain. Nothing except *his* voice.

"I can smell the sweat on your skin," he says, utilizing his skills of perception the way an assassin would a knife. To reinforce that comparison, the blindfold obscuring his vision is the same ebony shade as his suit, helping him cut a chilling figure against the blood-colored backdrop. "If you are nervous, we can leave. I'm sure I can devise another form of entertainment."

"N-No." The appearance of an easy out makes me shudder —this man, despite how short a time I've known him, doesn't strike me as the merciful type. More devilish if anything.

Because we've made a deal, he and I. It's only fitting that he brought me to Hell in order to honor that pact.

To be fair, his version of Hell is a stylish affair. Scarlet walls enclose a private booth resembling one that might be found in an opera house. Admittedly, an opera house that stars naked performers writhing upon black silken sheets rather than a stage.

In a sick way, there's beauty in it all.

Down below, two men and a woman lie entwined, their pale limbs entangled. Hoarse groans allude to their activity, but as far as I can tell, there's been no penetration. Yet. A strange detail to notice with a madman seated beside me.

Fully aware of him, I sense my inner thighs tense in a way that makes me stiffen and cross them tighter.

"I'm fine," I lie. "And I laid out my terms. It's only fair that you get to specify yours."

Like "dinner" here, again.

The first time he brought me to this taboo venue, the layout was admittedly different: a single couple viewed through a sheet of glass. Tonight, shadowed balconies reveal the vague hints of other people watching from across this wide atrium. At a glance, I count six booths in total, all with a bird's-eye view of the trio, their occupants rapt at attention.

"I will admit," I whisper, "that when you mentioned sex, I wasn't aware that you meant in the context of…an orgy." God, I can barely spit that word out. I breathe it instead, a gasp tinged by so many connotations. Dirty. Disgusting. Debasing.

Least of all: My father wouldn't approve.

The man who, as of two days ago, I considered to be my father, at least. Maybe that stubborn fact is why I haven't left yet? Why I can't seem to take my eyes off the naked woman being pawed like a toy doll between two different men, either.

Spite.

At least she's enjoying her stint as a pawn.

"I won't insist on anything you are not comfortable with," Damien warns, a rather polite non-denial. "You will have the final say in that matter when it comes to it. This is merely a diversion."

"From the saga of Heyworth Thorne," I snipe. "I know he's been trying to contact me." And I've avoided every message, call, and text. Something tells me that Damien hasn't strived to be as ignorant as I have, however. "How many times has he called today? Let me guess, he apologized? Promised to buy me a pony if I forgive him for protecting the identity of the man who made my life a living hell for twenty years? Or perhaps a new dress?" The vitriol undercuts the sensual murmurs drifting from below, and I have enough sense to feel some semblance of guilt. I'm ruining the show. "I'm sorry—"

"Don't be ashamed of your anger, " Damien growls, displaying his uncanny knack for sensing my emotions, even as I try to ignore them. "You have every right to express it."

"Do I?" I tilt my head thoughtfully, blinking back a burning sting from my eyes.

The loss of a loved one is an awful, ripping kind of pain. I've suffered it before—and I should be able to survive anything after that.

But I was wrong. So *wrong*.

My birth parents were absentee, barely imprinted in my memory—but Heyworth Thorne is my *father*. My mentor. My protector. My hero.

And beneath his well-crafted mask, he is little more than a fraud.

And a liar.

"Several," Damien says, shrugging the question off. Before I can command him to elaborate, he inclines his head toward the balcony. A not-so-subtle reference to the high-pitched moan emanating from below. "I must admit I'm curious as to the act encouraging our current soundtrack. Would you kindly narrate?"

I lean forward just enough to view the trio again. "They're fingering the woman," I dryly convey. "It looks rather uncomfortable, if I do say so myself—"

"Oh?" He laughs while copying my movements, his breath on my throat. "Do add some more theatrics to your descriptions, Ms. Thorne. I would like to visualize the scene, if you will. Is it one finger or two?"

I stiffen. Only he could pleasantly request something so obscene yet make it seem tempting to comply.

"They're…positioning her," I say. "On her hands and knees. The taller one is looming over her from behind and—"

"Ah, but what is she feeling?" As if such a thing could be discerned just at a glance.

Surprisingly, I think it can be as the woman in question arches her back into the taller man while brushing her fingers along the chest of the other.

"She's not ashamed," I hear myself croak. "I think…she's enjoying it."

"Is that so?" He's even closer, his scent flooding my nostrils with every breath I take. Wine. Cologne. Sin. My eyelids flutter as my gaze darts from the show to him and back again. "How could someone *enjoy* something so vulgar?"

"Her eyes are wide," I admit. "She's trembling. Moaning. I suppose you can hear the rest."

"That I can."

I turn in time to catch a flash of teeth as he grins. But just as quickly, a frown replaces the expression.

"I'm afraid our entertainment may be cut short."

"Huh?" I look behind us and find a hostess entering the booth, her teeth clenched.

She crosses to Damien and leans down to murmur something into his ear.

"I see," he replies, reaching for his cane. Extending his hand toward me, he nods to the door. "I was correct. After you."

"What's going on?" I warily place my hand on his and allow him to pull me along after the hostess, but he doesn't offer up an explanation. Near the mouth of the lobby, I deduce the reason for this unceremonious interruption all on my own.

Two police officers are guarding the door, glaringly out of place. Their twin stern expressions fixate on me simultaneously and one of them advances, his hand extended. "Miss Thorne?"

"Yes," I croak. "Can I help you?"

The two share a look. "Have you heard from your father recently?" the first one asks.

My heart falls into my stomach. "Is something wrong? Did something happen—"

"No," the man says quickly. "But he seems to be... concerned for your welfare."

"My welfare?" My brows furrow. "He didn't—"

"As you can see, she is safe and sound," Damien smoothly says before I can complete my suspicion out loud. "We apologize for the confusion, officers. Goodnight."

His careful tone implies the worst-case scenario. Like the fact that these officers didn't randomly show up to a sex club for the hell of it. They had been sent here.

For me.

"He called you, didn't he?" I demand of the nearer officer, who looks back at his partner. "My father?"

"We're just doing our duty, ma'am." A confirmation if there ever was one.

"Well, you can tell my *father*…" I grit my teeth over that word and choke it down. "*Heyworth Thorne.* You can tell him to stop contacting me. I'm fine."

"And you feel safe?" the other officer inquires, his eyes darting in Damien's direction. "Your father would like you to give him a call if you can. Just to reassure him that you're okay."

"Why?" I demand. But then another, more pointed question escapes. "Or what?"

Isn't the answer obvious?

"He wants you to arrest me, doesn't he?" I suspect, my voice breaking. "Or commit me, or whatever you can do to lock me away—"

"Juliana." Damien's hand lands over my shoulder. Even I know how insane I sound out loud. Paranoid. Irrational.

Days of obsessing over Heyworth's next move might do that to a person.

"You can tell him to go fuck himself," I hiss. "Tell him to—"

"I believe you have witnessed more than enough to be assured that Ms. Thorne is perfectly safe, as well as in her right mind," Damien says over me. "If you please."

When he touches my arm again, I have enough sense to follow, allowing him to guide me into another section of the shadowy lobby. Then through a door and into a small sitting room.

"That will be all," Damien says to the attendant, who scurries off. "Breathe," he commands me. "Getting upset now would only play into Thorne's hands."

I hate that he's right. That he can read me—and my father —so damn well. Like pawns on a well-studied chessboard. That's all we are to him really. Mere pieces in a giant game.

"You think like him," I croak, tearing my hands through my hair, desperate to keep them from shaking—it doesn't help. Helpless, I tug at the sleeves of my coat instead, straightening it over my black cocktail dress. He suggested formal attire for tonight's engagement—a bit of irony all things considered. My life is in shambles, but at least I'm well dressed for the occasion. "Always about appearances and propriety, and—"

"My reputation doesn't depend on you," Damien argues. "Frankly, we haven't been publicly linked, so I have no stake in ensuring the paparazzi doesn't capture a front-page story of you having a meltdown in a private club. So scream if you so choose. Rant. I will not judge you."

God, it's the wrong thing for him to say. Patient. Understanding.

Disarming.

"I would rather you be an ass right now," I admit. "It would be easier to be furious."

And I need to stay angry. Bitter. Callous.

Because if I can't…

"Forget the rest of the world." Like a wall of muscle, every contour of Damien hardens against me from behind. "If you don't mind, I'd rather we return to the show. Your sanitized narration has grown on me—"

"Is that what you want from me?" I ask.

His silence intrigues me, overriding the ache in my chest—for now. Like a drowning victim presented with a life rope, I latch onto it.

"Want to *do* to me, I mean. F-Fuck me in front of a room of people like some kind of pathetic porn—"

"I believe you weren't paying close enough attention, Ms. Thorne," he scolds, his lips grazing my jaw, a whisper of lethally soft flesh. "There is nothing pathetic about that woman. She holds all of the power in that instance. I would ask you not deride her method to express her empowerment. However, these excursions are diversions meant to occupy your attention. Nothing more."

"Diversions." It's as if tasting the word out loud unlocks the hidden meaning. Perhaps I ignored it until now. Here, in his private fantasy club, Heyworth Thorne would never dare follow. In fact, there is only one way anyone knew where to find us at all, I suspect. "Did Julio direct the police here?" I ask, referring to his lead bodyguard.

An uncharacteristic grunt escapes him. Then he sighs. "I have *friends* in law enforcement, shall we say. Your father has been persistent—belligerent, even. To placate him, they threatened to mount a more...public search. This way, they can be satisfied with seeing you safe and whole. For now. And the police chief can't use your association with me as fodder for his son's political machinations."

I raise an eyebrow. "And you didn't warn me?"

"Would you have come?" he inquires. "Would you have stayed?"

"I... Damn him." Ignoring his question, I refocus my irritation on the one person who deserves it. "Damn him—"

"But can you blame him? You have been avoiding him for two days."

"Don't pretend you care." Only as the words leave my mouth do I realize how ungrateful they sound. "I'm sorry. I just mean... After everything he put me through, the silent treatment isn't the worst method of revenge I could resort to."

What are a few days of shunning in comparison to over twenty years of lies? Deception designed to make me believe my best friend's killer was an unknown assailant. A specter. A shadow. When all along...he defended the man in court. He knows his identity. And even now, he has yet to tell me.

All to protect his pride.

"Have you learned anything?" I ask Damien, turning to face him. "About Simon?"

"I'm afraid not." He shakes his head. "The records are proving harder to track down than expected. But when I do discover anything at all, I'll alert you immediately."

"Thank you." I squeeze my eyes shut, even though it's futile around him. He may not be able to see my tears, but he can sense them. Smell them. I tremble as what feels like his thumb swipes at a fresh bead of liquid, wicking it away.

"I *will* keep looking," he promises. "In the meantime... Let me take you home—"

"No." Opening my eyes, I turn away from him and find myself nearing the threshold of the hallway. This place is so strange when given more scrutiny. Private. Discreet. Yet within these walls, anything but takes place. How strange that, of all potential hiding places, he would let the police find us here—because I have no doubt in my mind that they wouldn't be here otherwise. "Don't you value your privacy? I mean, if one of those officers decides to leak to the press that you were found in this place..."

"They could," he says. "Or perhaps, they *would* if I hadn't had Julio educate them on the strict privacy guidelines of this establishment before bringing them here. I've also ensured that their chief is aware to remind them. Though it was only a matter of time before they came here looking regardless."

Such a harmless statement reminds me eerily of the tensing of a trap readying to spring. Like a good lamb to the slaughter, I blindly step within its snare. "Why?"

"Because I own it," he explains. "And while its true purpose is private and its clientele strictly guarded, public documents are alas public. Though I did have the officers come in through a private entrance, preventing any unnecessary dramatics."

Which sounds like a lot of trouble to go through for a welfare check.

"Why not just take me home? Unless… You wanted them to find me here specifically. Or, to be blunter, you wanted *Heyworth Thorne* to know I was here. With you."

At a sex club.

His smile should unsettle me more than it does. "If I admitted as much, would that bother you?"

The bastard. He makes it sound so casual, as if he's truly offering me a legitimate choice.

But I've never had a choice, have I?

"You and my father can play your mind games," I tell him tiredly. "But…"

"But?"

"Don't ever do this again. Manipulate me like a pawn. I'm tired of power plays. I'm tired of being controlled. I would like to be in charge of my own damn life for once, if that's not too much to ask."

He nods. "*Sí.* I apologize if I have offended you."

"No…" I'm partly alarmed to find that he hasn't. Not entirely. Overall, my ex-father will learn tonight that I am at a sex club with Damien Villa of all people. How unfortunate that, all appearances aside, our visit has been rather platonic thus far.

Merely a three-way orgy starring a woman being fingered.

"What you said, about the woman being in control," I start, licking my lips. "What did you mean? How could someone possibly be in control in that situation?"

Such a scenario is the pure antithesis to everything I grew up believing about power. Like that it should be carefully controlled and kept on a leash. Never relished or flaunted.

"Do you feel in control now?" he counters. "You are constantly ogled by hundreds, if not thousands of people, hounding your every waking moment, waiting for a single flaw to pounce upon. I can only imagine how exhausting that could feel."

"I do feel powerless," I admit. "I am never in control—"

"And yet *that* woman is in an environment where she can feel safe. Where all who enter come for her. She sets the tone, the pace. Without her enjoyment, there is no… entertainment, shall we say. Her partners, the audience are at her mercy. She wields her power over the entire damn room, whether the occupants admit as much or not."

"And do you want to do that to me?" I wonder for the second time. "Put me on display?"

"No." His hesitation is even more apparent in the careful clearing of his throat. "I am not sure it is the type of control you would enjoy having."

"Why not?" I cross my arms over my chest, envisioning his potential replies. "I'm too much of a prude? I'm too weak? Too sheltered—"

"You are too *haunted*," he clarifies. "Laying yourself bare in front of strangers may be an experience you are not ready for. I will, however, take you up on your first suggestion." He steps forward, coming to my side. "Allow me to take you home."

"No." I shake my head even as I take the hand he's extended toward me and fall into step with his pace. "Not there."

Because police or not, I know Heyworth. He will have the SWAT team waiting to ambush my suite at the Lariat hotel the second I step inside it.

"Take me… Oh, I don't know." My temples ache, making it hard to settle on one of the many hotels within the city. Which one would my father—or the paparazzi—most likely overlook? "The Harrison?" I guess, thinking out loud. "Or maybe the Madison?"

"If I may make a suggestion," Damien murmurs. "I know someplace neither your father nor anyone else could enter. Not even the police."

"Oh?" It sounds too tempting. Another trap? "Where?" I ask, taking the bait regardless. Then, from the corner of my eye, I catch his teeth flash in a sinful, savoring smile.

"I believe it would perhaps be more impressive if I just showed you."

TWO

utterflies unfurl within my stomach as his driver pulls up in front of a building I vaguely recognize in the darkness. Multicolored streetlights illuminate an impressive skyscraper—one sporting an incredible glass greenhouse on the roof and owned by the man sitting stoically beside me.

"You can stay with me," he says, dropping all pretense. "My suite is large enough for you to have a section of rooms to yourself. If it makes you feel more comfortable, I will agree to stay within mine—"

"Considering you bought my virginity for all intents and purposes, you sure are"—I mull over the right phrase—"beating around the bush."

He laughs. "How crudely apt, Ms. Thorne. Though I *do* fully intend to collect on my half of our wager," he says with a fitting hint of malice. "But I believe my future plans may have a better reception if I tread carefully."

"Fine." I unbuckle my seat belt and reach for the door. Before I even touch the handle, Julio opens it from the outside.

Given the lack of a doorman and keycard entry, I assume this is yet another private entrance. Inside, a narrow black hallway leads to an elevator, but rather than the one for the roof, Damien strikes the button for the floor below it.

My heart pounds as the doors finally part and I follow him out. Unsurprisingly, the décor is black, but the floor plan is more open than I expected, given his penchant for shadowy, decadent places. A modest living room consists of black leather chairs and chaises positioned in front of a massive window displaying a view of the city. Beyond that is an open kitchen with bar seating, a dining room, and then two hallways that branch off in different directions.

Damien heads right. "This is the way to your suite," he explains, throwing the term out as easily as some people might discuss a spare pair of shoes. "You should have everything you need. If not, Julio or I will see to it."

I hold my breath as I glance over his shoulder into the first of the rooms: a beige décor sets it apart from his typical color scheme.

"Let me guess: You told your designer to have free rein in this section of the penthouse?" I snipe.

"Oh, no." He laughs and shakes his head. "Far from it. I told her to design a room that Juliana Thorne would be mildly comfortable dwelling within."

I can't tell if he's joking or not. Neither can I muster up the energy to ask. Instead, I step into the room, spotting all the little details that would prove his remarks twistedly true. The décor, disregarding the beige, mimics that of my suite at the Lariat: simple though luxurious furniture and an open floor plan. On its face, it's the style someone would assume the heiress daughter of a powerful judge might be used to.

"Impressive," I admit, aware of him advancing on me with slow, precise steps. "Though the color scheme is a bit more muted than I would expect."

"Oh?" His chuckle tickles the back of my neck, lingering even as his steps retreat toward the hall. "I hope you find the bedroom equally as…comforting. I'm afraid you may describe it as far too conservative for a woman of your talents. Alas, it should suffice. Goodnight, Ms. Thorne."

Wary, I continue through the suite as his steps fade, inching toward the room I assume the bedroom in question to be.

For a second, I forget that Damien isn't in earshot as I mutter, "Very funny. You think you know me so well."

Maybe he does considering he supposedly designed a room damn near tailored to make me feel entirely out of my element. Conservative my ass. The walls are red, the floors a plush, sensual black. A luxurious bed draped in red satin sheets serves as the most intimidating focal point.

And on the ceiling is an enormous gilded mirror. Because of course there is.

So the blind man has jokes. Very funny. I laugh to prove I'm unaffected as I shed my jacket and brace myself over the edge of the mattress. But without him here…

I don't have a barrier from the guilt. Not the pain or the crushing realization that the past twenty years of my life have been one monstrous lie. Only one person holds the answers.

Why, why, why?

As I fish my cell phone from my purse, I'm determined to discover that very fact once and for all.

"Thorne residence," a gruff voice demands from the other end of the line. "How can I assist—"

"It's Juliana," I say over who must be a bodyguard. "Put me through."

"Of course, Ms. Thorne."

Not even a second later, a familiar voice drips into my ear. "Juliana? Sweet pea, please tell me what is going on—"

"Why don't you tell me?" I counter. "Starting with who exactly he is: Simon. You've known all this time, haven't you? Who he really is?"

"Darling…" The background noise shifts and mutes behind him. He must have secluded himself into another room. "We need to discuss this in person. Please. I've been worried sick about you. Come home and we can—"

"If we talk, it will be somewhere public," I blurt. "The Lariat. This time, maybe you can leave out the police?"

An audible grunt escapes him. "Darling, can you really blame me?"

"Tomorrow morning at nine," I snap. "Be there and…and tell me everything. I mean it. Or…"

I can't even say it. *Or consider me your daughter no longer.*

"I will," he insists. "Just tell me where you are. That you're safe. The police are—"

I hang up and crawl beneath the sheets before I can regret contacting him in the first place. It's pathetic how your entire identity can be wrapped up within one person. Their aura. Their persona.

If that's stripped away, they become a stranger, and you…

You become a shadow.

THREE

I creep from Damien Villa's lair to the first floor of the building with him none the wiser—or so I think.

A man's lurking near the mouth of the building's lobby. As the elevator doors part, he steps forward, and my knees buckle. Tall. Golden skin. Cropped raven hair. He could be Damien…if it weren't for his whole, dark-brown eyes.

"Mateo Villa," I croak, inching back as the elevator doors close behind me.

"Juliana Thorne," he coldly replies. "How strange to find you here, of all places…" In lieu of his brother's trademark suit, he's wearing a pair of jeans and a leather jacket. A mocking half-smile sets him further apart from Damien, but a steely nature reinforces his gaze, leaving me uneasy. "Though I shouldn't be surprised," he adds. "My brother did pay for the privilege to play with you in private."

"Privilege?" I fight to keep my chin in the air.

"*Sí.*" He scoffs, his mouth quirked. "He didn't tell you? Maybe I should have pressed him for more in our bargain?"

"What do you want?" I consider running. Calling for help. Before I can make the decision, he turns and strolls toward a hallway.

"Don't bother calling my brother to heel," he calls back. "And as for what I want? Why to warn you, of course." He pauses and cocks his head.

"Of what?" I croak when he doesn't elaborate. "Trust and believe I'll report every threat to the police."

"My brother is a dangerous man, Ms. Thorne. You should do your best to remember that. He may put on his charming act around you"—he flicks his gaze up to my face and chuckles—"but don't be fooled by his blindness. You must have given him quite the roll in the hay. I've never seen him so fucking whipped."

Heat floods my cheeks though I fight to keep my chin in the air. "E-Excuse me?"

"I'm surprised he got much use out of you, all things considered." He nods pointedly toward my body in general. "You aren't his type. Not a trophy, I think. Just a toy for his amusement. One he isn't inclined to share though. Not yet. He damn near threatened to kill me if I touched you. But still." He shrugs and heads farther down the hall, briefly turning to toss his parting words my way. "I pity you. Even I can find it in my heart to warn an easy mark. Your father is a selfish, moral-less cunt, but Damien thrives on vengeance. Don't trust him. Considering that just by touching you he's spitting on Mathias' memory, the *hijueputa* has no loyalty."

He retreats, and my blood runs cold, my heart solidifying into a painful lump in my chest. With difficulty, I ignore him and focus on the task at hand: escaping.

One fearful peek beyond the lobby reveals a familiar black car waiting for me along the curb. *Damn.* The moment I exit the building, Julio climbs from the vehicle and the jig is up.

"Good morning, Ms. Thorne," he declares, opening the door to the back seat. "Mr. Villa thought you might appreciate having him supply your transportation this morning." His stoic expression reveals nothing. I can't tell if he knows about my brush with Mateo—but I suspect that this "offer" isn't by coincidence, either.

"Does Mr. Villa have the room I stayed in bugged?" I ask without expecting an answer—because it's obvious. Given his track record, I wouldn't put another instance of espionage past him.

Luckily for Damien, I'm not in the mood to resist him this time. Mateo's little warning made it clear that navigating this uncertain landscape alone may not be in my best interest—especially where my father is concerned.

So I climb into the car without complaint, and minutes later, Julio deposits me in front of the private residential entrance of the Lariat, safe from any prying paparazzi. It's a short, unnerving trip up to my apartment.

But Heyworth is nowhere to be found.

Julio stands guard in the hallway while I wait, passing the time by alternating staring out the window and checking my phone. A quick scan of the top news stories doesn't reveal any unusual traffic jams—but a flashing headline chills me to the core.

The Borgetta Murder Case: five people connected dead within a month of overturned conviction.

Perhaps my father's security detail took extra precautions this morning, thus delaying him over thirty minutes?

After nearly an hour, I finally breakdown and call.

"Thorne residence," the same man from last night announces.

"Where is he?" I demand.

"Mr. Thorne is…indisposed at the moment. I'm afraid he'll have to reschedule."

"Reschedule?"

The line goes dead without further explanation and my heart twists inside my chest. Could something be wrong?

Or perhaps something more important has come up. More important than mending fences with me. A coveted interview? A donor meeting? The possibilities mount and each one feels increasingly plausible.

Heyworth pushed me aside for yet another political calculation.

It's nothing new, but this time…

Tears spill down my cheeks like liquid fire as I tear into the hallway, heedless of who may be spying from the shadows.

"Ms. Thorne?" Julio calls after me as I surge into an opening elevator. "I suggest we take the private exit—"

The elevator doors close behind him and part seconds later to reveal the lobby, where a sea of flashing cameras stops me dead in my tracks. Reporters—too damn many of them to be here by accident. Panic renders me frozen as a million shouted questions descend in a barrage of clashing voices.

"Miss Thorne! Is it true that you are in a relationship with Damien Villa, the brother of the man your father sentenced to death?"

"Miss Thorne, care to comment?"

"Juliana! Do you have any comment on the fact that people related to your father's case have died recently—"

"Juliana!" A balding man with a beer gut comes from nowhere to shove a microphone in my face. "Your father has been accused of racial bias. Given your birth mother's heritage, did you witness anything of the sort growing up?"

I don't know what happens. One second, I'm staring down at my trembling fingers. The next, my knuckles are connecting with something alarmingly flesh-like and blood is flying through the air. Alarmed cries go up as the reporter crouches, clutching his nose.

"You crazy bitch!" he shrieks as he, and the rest of the world, come back into focus.

Crazy bitch. Those two words are all I hear as I push through the mass of people and somehow make it out of the building. Blindly, I run, crossing traffic and intersections until I reach some semblance of quiet what seems like an eternity later. A park, I assume, judging from close-set trees and scattered benches.

Here, I can hear myself think. About how much of an idiot I am. Gullible. Desperate. Pathetic.

And worthless, apparently. I sure hope Daddy's meeting or television appearance was worth it.

At least I keep it together until I find a bench tucked within a copse of trees. Only now do I finally break, burying my face in my hands.

I don't hear him until it's too late. By the time I stiffen at the sound of approaching footsteps, he's already close enough to swipe his finger along my cheek.

"You know how to make quite the scandal," he murmurs, his accent especially pronounced.

Despite the overall polished elegance conveyed by his black coat and scarlet scarf, he's breathing more quickly than usual. A bead of sweat glints on his jaw. Like he rushed here?

"The reporter is pressing charges, or at least he *was*," Damien adds. "May I?" With what I presume is a practiced motion, he finds the back of the bench with one hand and uses it as a guide to lower himself onto it.

I doubt he's omniscient enough to find me without help—and sure enough, I spot Julio in the distance, muttering into a headset, feeding his boss my location, I suspect.

"A rather dull man from a paper few read anyway," Damien continues as if uninterrupted. "A bit of money to pad his next check and an inside scoop on some tawdry celebrity scandal and the man changed his mind."

"Why?" I demand, swiping at my face with my sleeve.

"Hmm." He tilts his head. "I assume because he enjoys money and notoriety—"

"No, I mean…why help me?" Is what Mateo claimed true? He bargained to keep even his brother from me?

"Why?" A frown distorts that stern, beautiful mouth, confusing me further. "Unless you've forgotten, you yourself laid out the terms of our agreement."

That I did.

Stay with me.

Protect me.

"Then you should have no trouble humoring me," I say. "Or with telling me the truth."

"Of course," he says without a hint of hesitation. "You only need to ask."

"You spied on me last night. You knew I was meeting with my father."

"*Sí.*" He cocks his head without an ounce of shame. "Seeing as I appointed myself head of your security, I feel no need to deny that."

Touché. Once more, I'm forced to admit that he has a point.

"Did you know that he didn't show?" I demand. "If so, then tell me. Did someone powerful come along and make him an offer he couldn't refuse?" I force a smile while telling myself I can handle any explanation. But my stomach churns more the longer Damien's silence extends. It's not out of ignorance, I suspect. He's hiding something. "Just tell me."

"I'm not sure," he concedes. "Just that he canceled all appointments for the day."

"You don't think something's wrong, do you?" The concern in my voice isn't fake. Heyworth Thorne may be many things. But for twenty years, he was my father. Go figure, those emotions can't be shaken overnight. "Maybe I should go to the house?" I start to stand.

"I can have Julio take you there now," Damien suggests without moving. "Merely say the word."

"Or it could be a trick," I find myself blurting, lowering beside him again. "Lure me to the house. Ambush me with the police present. Declare me mentally unfit. Have me committed—"

"Well, you did physically assault an innocent, prying journalist," Damien dryly interjects. "In the midst of cursing you to hell and back, the man did admit that you have a decent right hook."

I laugh, alarmed by how real it sounds. A real laugh in this shit-storm of a morning.

"Can I ask you for something else?"

He doesn't even bother to answer me this time. A stern grunt is all the encouragement I need to confess.

"I…I want to forget everything about today." My father. Mateo. The press. "You can pick the distraction." Even as the words leave my mouth, I know how dangerous they sound. "Just take me somewhere far away where I don't have to think. Please."

"A brave request." He stands and murmurs into his headset, "Julio, bring the car around *por favor*." To me, he offers his hand and helps me to my feet. "That I can do."

Of all places he could take me, he fittingly picks one of the last I'd assume.

His waterfront studio. The place where he sketched me for the first time on his wooden table. Naked. Today, a blank canvas dominates an easel placed strategically in the center of that same room. Beside it is a flat marble slab with a mattress covered in a black sheet balanced on top.

A brave request, he said. Now, I'm starting to realize why.

"Strip," Damien commands, shedding his own coat, which he tosses onto a leather chair near the entrance. "You can leave the dress on the floor. I assure you it's clean. Then, we can begin."

"You plan to paint me?" My gaze settles on the marble slab and then the easel set up beside it.

"You sound skeptical," Damien points out, pouncing on my unease. "Not quite what you had in mind?"

He doesn't seem disappointed. If anything… amused, like a master puppeteer waiting for his pretty little doll to notice her strings.

"Lying still for a long period of time utterly motionless isn't exactly conducive to helping me forget." Even still, my hands graze the front of my coat. Slowly, I undo the first button.

"Motionless?" Damien echoes, tapping his chin with an extended finger. "Who said I would use the drug this time? In fact, I will offer you a choice."

"A choice?" Intrigued, I track his trek across the room.

When he reaches the marble slab, his cane in hand, he bends in an elegant motion, lifting something from a shelf built into the side of the structure. A tray, I see as I come closer. On it are a few assorted objects. A mirror, a small box, a swath of black silk…

"A blindfold?" I question.

"*Sí*," Damien says, his mouth quirked. "You may pick between it and the drug—"

"The blindfold," I blurt while snatching up the strip of silk. I'm relieved for reasons I can't explain as the fabric settles into the palm of my hand. "Now what?"

"Now…" He turns his attention to the small box and lifts the lid, revealing the round objects lying on a bed of red velvet. "Pearls," he explains. "Harvested by hand and chosen for quality. They are damn near priceless; I can assure you of that. Each one is exquisitely unique."

"Oh?" It's hard to keep the awe from my tone. Only a man like him would have priceless items lying around out in the open, their purpose unknown. I tentatively finger one bead, impressed by the quality. "Are you planning on bribing me with a necklace, Mr. Villa?"

"Something like that." His deep, rumbling laugh sends tendrils of unease lancing through my blood. "You will lie back while I paint you," he explains, his tone professionally level. "I will place these pearls on your body and you must not allow them to move. Does that make for a fitting diversion?"

I swallow hard, intrigued despite myself. "And if they *do* fall off?"

He smiles, and I have never witnessed something so devastatingly beautiful. Rather than answer me right away, he extends his palm, and without being prompted further, I surrender the blindfold. As easily as if he's memorized every inch of my body, he reaches out and finds my cheek.

"Turn around, sweet girl." His use of the endearing term sets my nerves on the edge of a cliff.

When I comply, he draws the silk over my eyes, using my ears as a guide. After tying the knot, he steers me back until what I assume to be the ledge of the platform brushes my hip.

"Every pearl that falls is one I will be allowed to use," he says, casually picking up the thread of our previous conversation. "As I see fit."

"In what way?" I question.

Subtle sounds are all I have to discern his next movements. A soft click, as if he propped his cane against an edge of the platform, followed by the creak of the leather-topped stool placed halfway between the platform and the easel. It makes sense. From that position, both are within his reach—as will I be.

"In a way that will allow me to explore your body in a manner entirely separate from my art."

Heat sears my cheeks. A nun could hear the innuendo in his tone—and he's done so well to disguise it until now: the restrained lust oozing from him, as tantalizing as his cologne. A part of me shivers in response. Flinches. I'm painfully aware of the thin fabric of my dress whispering over my skin.

"Have I startled you, Ms. Thorne?" he wonders innocently. A soft hiss makes me imagine him picking up the brush, dipping it into paint before testing a streak over the canvas. "Perhaps you find this proposed diversion too stimulating? We can skip the blindfold, if that appeases you."

"No. In fact, I think you have a deal, Mr. Villa." I wrench my coat open, fiddling with the buttons as I go. Once it's off, I toss it aside and shed my dress, feeling the chill in the room. My nipples tighten as I wad my panties up and discard that as well. "Now what?"

"Lie down." His voice has deepened. Gone is the mocking, playful edge, and I can't stop my arms from flinching toward my breasts, despite his lack of sight. An artist has replaced the powerful, reclusive billionaire—but he's a more dangerous animal. One who communicates with grit in his tone and an authoritative aura. "On your back," he prompts as I feel for the platform and perch myself on the edge of it. "Don't worry about positioning your limbs. I will arrange them for you."

An ominous sentence if there ever was one.

"Arrange?" I can't resist parroting as I run my fingers along the silken sheets, testing their quality: luxurious. "You make it sound more in-depth than painting."

"*Sí.*" A wistful sigh rips from his throat. "It always is…"

"Ah, how could I forget? You've done this before."

Painting naked women is a pastime that's garnered him acclaim. Though it's the first time in a while that he's referred to his other subjects—a deliberate tactic, I suspect. Deciphering his reasons why is like playing an elaborate game of chess with a master far out of my league.

So I forge a change in subject.

"I'm lying down." Twisting, I lift my legs and lower myself onto the platform. "So when do the pearls come into play?" I ask, sounding bolder than I feel.

"Now."

I sense him stand again and my ears strain to catch his every movement. There is a practiced grace to how he moves, supposedly pivoting on his feet to navigate the slender path between his stool and the platform. From this angle, I have no idea where he's positioned. My only clues are the nuanced shifts in the air. His breathing. His scent.

"Are you ready?" Gone is the smug mocking from his voice. I picture his nostrils flaring, his tongue flicking along his lower lip.

With what I suspect is another practiced motion, he finds the tray near my hip and noisily drags it closer to him, allowing the edge to brush my skin so I can feel every single inch.

Tiny pings make me assume that the pearls are colliding with the sides of the tray. Each delicate click sends my heart surging just a bit faster. There are too many possibilities for him to implement the words he said. Use the pearls to explore me. But how?

I'm so lost in thought that I almost miss the moment he seizes one of the ivory balls between his thumb and his forefinger: the only solution I can envision when the tiny noises suddenly go silent. I can almost see him rolling his chosen pearl between his fingers as if memorizing every slight flaw in its surface. Satisfied, he'd cock his head, a dangerous grin shaping his mouth.

"Do you want to place them initially, or should I?"

"Is that a trick question?" I counter, resorting to the only weakness of his I can use to my advantage: his blindness. "Just tell me where you want them and I'll—"

He laughs. "Oh, I'm sure I could manage. Your hip," he announces before the silk pad of a finger brushes along my side, persistent even as I jump. "Your stomach. Your navel. Should I utilize this spot in particular?"

I shiver as he flicks the dip in my belly. Rather than move on, he lingers, imparting his heat into my skin merely to prove a point.

"Yes, here," he declares before replacing his touch with the unmistakable round shape of a pearl.

Panic spreads down my spine like wildfire as the slight weight settles there precariously. One wrong move and it's gone.

"And if it falls?" I struggle to ask while keeping my stomach flat.

He laughs again, but the sound is an octave deeper. "I'll let you imagine what the consequence may be."

"B-But—"

"Next one," he declares, cutting me off. The hiss of silk and flesh teases my ears as he presumably rummages through the contents of the tray to retrieve yet another pearl.

"Open your mouth," he commands as the noise ceases.

"W-What?" Heat brushes my cheek, easily finding my mouth—his thumb, I think. He teases my lower lip with the hardened tip of a nail. "Why?"

"Just open."

My lips part on command and I'm rewarded with the hint of salt. From his *thumb*. The rigid shape is recognizable as my tongue skims the ridges and whirls on the pad of it. With every tentative lick, my stomach twists into knots, registering his unique taste. Sweat. Sin. His finger withdraws before I can decipher more, and something new replaces it. Smooth with a slightly gritty surface, not completely round. And…

It's wet, tainted with flavor. The sinful taste triggers my memory as heat ignites near my belly: expensive wine like the kind he owns. A dangerous thought worms its way into my skull, robbing the air from my lungs. Did he taste this before giving it to me?

The pearl withdraws before I muster up the strength to decide. For a painful few seconds, he remains silent.

"Perhaps here, next?" he murmurs as a soft touch teases the space between my breasts.

I gasp, remembering the first pearl before it's too late. Moisture paints my skin in the wake of the second pearl, leaving a path that cools instantly in the air. I shiver as he guides it up…over…

There's no disguising my body's instinctive reaction. A low hum taints the air as the pearl meets the stiffened peak of my nipple.

"Here?" he wonders thickly before rolling the pearl down my breast. There he leaves it, balanced on my breastbone.

He's quiet again, only his breathing gives me any clue where he is—more distant as if he's moved near my feet. The next moment, his touch is back, at my ankle this time. I can feel the heat of his hand, but only a newer pearl contacts my skin, gliding up my leg. I feel all its imperfections, its dents as it grazes my calf. It's surprisingly gritty like sand, teasing the flesh on my knee.

"Here?" he murmurs, lingering again.

My lower half trembles, muscles tense to ensure the other pearls don't move.

"Or here?"

Coldness swipes along my inner thigh, inching higher…

I barely register the unnerving sensation of the small bead between my legs before a firmer touch continues its original path. I have no trouble naming the culprit: his hand. The individual shape of every finger sends my senses spiraling. My spine stiffens, aching to arch—into him? Away from him? The thinnest shred of pride keeps me still, a slave to his touch. One by one, he spreads his fingers over my hip. Slowly…so damn slowly, they dance across my pelvis, stopping just short of the thatch of curls at the base of my abdomen.

And another pearl settles, jarring my dazed thoughts.

"Last one." Alarm sets in as his finger caresses a path up my throat and finds my lips. "Open," he commands again.

This time, I definitely taste salt as his finger glides across my tongue. "Close."

Once my lips meet, a gentle pressure seals them shut—the final pearl.

"There." He turns back to his canvas and the stool creaks beneath his weight. "Now we can begin. I hope you are comfortable, Juliana?"

He chuckles in that slow, callous way when I don't answer.

"Good. Now that I have your full attention, we can discuss in detail what I plan to do to you. When I finally decide to take what I am owed."

My lips twitch and the pearl slips—thank God it doesn't fall. It's certain now; the man is evil. Pure, unadulterated evil.

"I'm sure you've wondered about it," he taunts. "Obsessed over every little detail—you may let your gilded world control every aspect of your life, but you still can't stand it. And yet you haven't asked me."

So he has noticed my silence on that topic. Has he been waiting for me to broach it first?

The pearl feels like a lead weight, keeping me silent. And like a true torturer, he knows exactly how to twist the knife.

"Shall I tell you?" That dangerous chuckle rumbles from him again. "Though I'm tempted to let you stew on it. There are so many ways to rob you of that one shred of innocence you cling to—because you *have* clung to it. I know you've dated before." He throws it off like a casual observation, but it conveys so much more. Like the fact that he's delved into more than just my past. Perhaps he's spied on more than my intimate moments as well. "All powerful, pretty men, none of whom last the month with you. And not because *they* leave *you*," he adds, proving my suspicions correct. "You never let them in. Not to your apartment. Not even the damn building. You've built a wall between the world and your private life and I doubt you even know how to break it. Because of him."

He doesn't say the name. I flinch regardless—and the round bead on my breastbone shifts, threatening to roll off. Holding my breath is the only way to keep it still.

"He hurt you, didn't he?" There's an uncharacteristic softness to his baritone. "In more ways than killing your friend."

No. I squeeze my eyes shut and inhale, heedless of the way the pearls on my body lurch in response. A frantic sound builds up in my throat but doesn't escape my mouth. Yet. A plea. *Please don't.*

"I'm not mocking you," he clarifies like it matters—but the gruff, bitter note in his voice makes me bite back a scoff. "Your limits. Your fears. *Those* are the things I must know before I can fully take what you wagered. I refuse to traumatize you, for lack of a better word. Despite what happens between us, I have no intention of harming you."

And perhaps that's why he claimed to be willing to offer up anything in advance. The price of my deepest, darkest secrets is one worth paying to a man like him.

So that he can use my past against me?

"I believe the best course of action would be to have you demonstrate for me," he muses amid the scrape of the brush on the canvas. "Where to touch you. How. Exhibition seems to be one of your defining traits. I'm sure you'd enjoy the experience more than I—"

"You're insane." *Ping!* The musical sound chimes a faint warning as my lips part again. "You wouldn't!"

"Wouldn't what?" he murmurs.

With my mouth free, I don't hold back. "Take me to your creepy little club," I spit hoarsely. "Make me...in front of—"

"You think I meant publicly? Oh, no. Some experiences should remain private between two individuals. Like how you sound in the throes of an orgasm. *Sí...*" A grated sound resonates in his throat. "The members of my club don't pay nearly enough to partake in that kind of entertainment."

"Why even own a club like that?" I spit without parsing the possession evident in that statement. A nefarious reason worms into my brain. "Do you participate in the 'entertainment' yourself perhaps? At an owner's discount?"

"*¿Qué?*" Another heartless laugh conveys he's anything but insulted. "No. I am afraid the true reason is rather boring, Ms. Thorne: leverage."

"How enterprising of you," I counter. "Naked, undisguised blackmail. There is a poetic irony to it."

"*Gracias,* though I'm not sure you fully appreciate what I mean. Humans are such strange creatures, you see. They'd give one man the absolute power to destroy their lives in a heartbeat, all for the promise of freedom to indulge in the most wicked of pastimes. It is quite the Faustian bargain."

"Leverage?" I echo. "That sounds more like blackmail. I thought you valued discretion and ensured privacy?"

"And I do," he insists, but I sense another half to that statement that he doesn't voice. *And I do...for now.* "But if you're wondering if I fuck the performers in my spare time, I'm afraid the answer is no."

"Why not?"

"You still don't understand me at all, do you?" He sounds so amused by the prospect. But maybe he's wrong in this case.

"Because you expect to gain something from every encounter," I answer before he can say anything else. "To learn something. For your art—"

"And I wonder how much I'll learn about you via this delicate, single pearl. Do drop another *por favor*."

The air in my lungs escapes in a gasp. Damn it. That's right. I've given him a victory already: one pearl lost. I'm suddenly aware of the remaining three balanced precariously on their respective positions.

"Hmmm." The floorboards protest as he stands.

I imagine him swiping his fingers along his chin. Specks of dark liquid most likely coat the tips. Paint. I can even smell it, sharp and chemical, melding with the amalgam of scents that enhance his persona.

Circling to my direction, he grasps where I suspect the tray of pearls to be. An array of soft clinking noises conjures an image of him fondling every round bead, looking for the perfect one. Despite the blindfold, I can almost see him as he finally raises his selection trapped between two fingers.

"Shall I make a confession?" he muses. "It's not every woman that I would allow to make demands of me. Flowers every day…"

He's referring to one of my delirious requests made in the aftermath of a world-altering betrayal.

"Those were *your* terms," I point out, fighting to keep every muscle still. "You said anything—"

"And I meant that. But I am sure you love a good bargain as much as I do, and I believe it would only be fair if I were to make a request in return."

My body twitches in response to his deepening baritone.

"So what do you say? I continue to send you your flowers. You perform a daily task of my request, and in return, you get to bargain something else from me."

"Like what?"

"By now, I'm sure you know the answer." He pauses for drama's sake and then rasps, "*Anything.*"

"Fine. Then whatever you're planning for when you take my… I-I have to agree to it," I propose in a rush. "You can't force me to—"

"I'll do you one better; I'll make you beg for it. Fair enough?" He waits for a reply that never escapes my throat. "As for now… I believe I am required to do something with my pearl."

Heat runs through me like a lance. *His* pearl. God, such a tiny object has never seemed so menacing.

"Do I have your permission, Ms. Thorne?"

He's serious. If I say no, I have no doubt he'll drop the pearl and leave—yet lord my fear over me in some way down the road. A man like him demands his payment. An eye for an eye.

Always.

"Y-Yes."

"Good."

I track a sudden series of movements coming from near the end of the pedestal.

"Do you want me to tell you what I plan to do?"

I nearly jump as his touch teases my lower lip yet again, urging me to open. "Y-Yes," I murmur against his fingertips.

"I feel a demonstration may be more…telling." He sounds closer, his scent strong enough to taste. All of him. "So do I have your permission to utilize a pearl as I see fit?"

"W-Wait." I jolt upright, braced on my elbows. Distant pings allude to the fact that the other pearls have fallen, but I can't even spare enough concern to truly despair. Damn, I almost wish he'd used the drug instead.

There's something about the idea of him hunched between my spread legs. I can hear every cadence in his breathing, slow and deliberate. Labored. He's disguising just how much he wants to touch me, but his finger twitching against my tongue betrays him. I doubt he's even aware of it. Wanting. This man can display the deepest emotions of others so easily.

He has no clue how much he himself can give away.

"And if I refuse?" I manage to whisper as my inner thighs twitch, aching to clamp together. "What if I say no?"

"You won't." His accent thickens with confidence. "You're too curious. Too daring for your own good. You want to know even more than I want to continue. So shall we both drop the pretense? *This* is what I plan to do with the goddamn pearl—"

His fingers slip between my legs, pressing against sensitive flesh. I jump, clawing at his forearms, as the unmistakable shape of the pearl toys near my entrance, guided by his swiping thumb. One flick of his wrist nudges it farther. Another pushes it *deeper*.

Explore, he said. The word he meant was *invade*.

And there is no escape. The broadness of his callused palm captures me, but the pearl is a terrifying bit of leverage, probing with the right amount of pressure. Too small. I feel him more than it, easing inside me.

And it is sin. Hell. He has me on a string, arching with every touch.

"Let the world see you like this?" he growls, his voice dripping into my ear, easily overpowering the pathetic gasps escaping my throat.

There's a method to his madness. His finger caresses me first. Then the pearl strikes a tense ball of nerves, making every thought in my brain go haywire. Explode. Unravel.

"Let them see you in the only way I cannot? Like hell. This is *mine*." He quirks his thumb, making my spine contract, manipulated like a marionette. "Your heavy pants, mine to taste. Your wails of ecstasy, mine to hear." He teases me with a second finger, spreading me open. "The tightening of every muscle just before you lose control, mine to feel. The scent of your arousal that lingers long after, mine to smell."

I can't stop what he unleashes within my body. A torrent of fire robs me of everything but sight. Feel. Sensation.

His taste is on my tongue, his mouth at my throat, his fingers inside me, thrusting so deep that it toes the edge of pain. Lust has a razor's edge with him. Too sharp.

He'll cut me with it.

Or kill me.

But the prospect of death by his hand is alarmingly tempting. There's no noise in this shadowy realm of pleasure. No secrets or lies to combat. The world fades as all the darkness gives way to blinding white. My brain separates from my body—all I know is that an unyielding strength supports me as I writhe through the tumult of ecstasy.

Until it's over.

Reality inevitably descends and I find myself panting against a stranger. A stranger who's murmuring into my ear, grated sinful things. "Wet for me… *Dios mío.*"

He's still touching me through the praises. Stroking. The pearl plays tag with the thickness of his finger. I'm full of him. Teased with his substitute. Full again.

Over, and over, and over…

"D-Damien." Rippling muscle serves as my only anchor as I curl my fingers, nails drawn. Anything to retaliate. But my attempts just make his touch all the bolder.

"You hold your breath when you're on the verge of coming," he grates against my throat. "So desperate for control. You don't want to scream—it feels that damn good."

Heat fans my lower lip. Both of mine part. His come down to devour them whole. The thickness of his tongue is a disturbing contrast to his thumb. He times his strokes so both thrust into me at the same time. I'm overwhelmed. Empty. Bursting.

"You don't want to moan," he grunts, drawing his mouth back. "So you bite your tongue. But I can't stand your silence. I won't coddle you. Shelter you. I can *give* to you, sweet girl. You only need to ask nicely."

Another kiss consumes any sound I might make. My hands leave his arms and move into his hair, grasping at the thick strands. He copies me, cupping my scalp, using it to deepen the contact between us. His teeth nip at my lip and the pain makes me reckless.

Reckless enough to bite him back. Grip him back. Push back, urging him inside me. Harder. Deeper.

Consequences no longer matter, neither do his calculated little plans.

In this moment, I need him like I've needed nothing else.

"Mr. Villa?"

A heavy knock on the door feels too surreal, like a random moment from a nightmare. I ignore it first, swatting it away like a buzzing fly—but Damien goes rigid, his lips still on mine.

Fury is palpable in the way he harshly exhales as he withdraws. "*Meirda.*"

Just like that, I'm back in my body. Back in the real world. Arched on a pedestal with Damien Villa's hand between my legs. He's already sliding his fingers away, taking the pearl with them.

It isn't until another knock echoes off the walls that I realize I'm not hallucinating. We've been interrupted. Within seconds, the world is a serious, shadowy place again. And the man in front of me is someone to never underestimate.

"You are to never disturb me," he bellows in a thunderous tone that radiates throughout the room. "In fact, I don't know whether or not to fire you—"

"It's urgent, sir," Julio replies, sounding muffled, as if he's speaking from behind the door, as calm as ever. "I apologize for the breach in protocol, but...I assumed you would want to hear it before Ms. Thorne had the chance to catch the news coverage."

News coverage? I undo the blindfold one-handed and blink, finding Damien scowling near the edge of the platform.

"Get dressed," he says before moving to the door.

I slip from the mattress and stoop for my dress and panties. Hunched away from Damien, I slip it on over my head, but he's already marching across the room, radiating rage with every thundering step.

"Are you dressed?" he barks at me.

I pull my coat on and fumble with the buttons. "Y-Yes."

He wrenches the door open, revealing Julio on the other end. The man leans toward him and murmurs into his ear.

"I see," Damien says, his tone degrees cooler. "Yes, I understand. You made the right call, as always."

Julio nods and presses something into Damien's hand. "Sir," he says before stepping back into the hall. He doesn't go far, I suspect.

"Juliana…" Damien extends his hand in my direction, revealing just what he's holding: my cell phone. "Call your stepmother."

"Diane?" Nerves unfurl in my stomach as I approach him, feeling too uneasy to voice my suspicions out loud.

Has my father made a more public plea this time? Accused me of being insane on national television? No, his reputation matters too much for such a stunt.

Right?

"What's wrong?" I take the phone and glance at the screen. There are four missed calls from my father's office and four more from Diane's direct cell—all within the span of an hour.

"Hello?" Diane picks up on the first ring. "Juliana?"

"What's going on?"

"Oh, thank God! I told him to tell you sooner, but he didn't want to worry you. And now I don't know what we're going to do. The doctors don't—"

"Slow down," I urge. "I don't understand. What's wrong?"

"Your father is in the hospital," she says. "He had a stroke. Juliana… It's not good. Please come…"

The phone falls from my grasp, sliding across the floor as the world dips in and out of focus. One minute, I'm standing; the next, I'm on my knees, supported only by a strong hand on my shoulder. Like an anchor, a gruff voice sinks through the chaos of my thoughts, tethering me to reality.

"I'll take you there," Damien says, though I don't even remember asking him to out loud, let alone saying anything. "I've got you."

FOUR

$\mathcal{E}$ven now, whenever I picture Heyworth Thorne, it's always as he was the day we met: a knight in shining armor, rescuing me from a nightmare. I'd been sedated that morning, three days after Simon's attack. Lying tucked beneath the stale, stiff blankets of a hospital bed, draped in tubes and wires meant to monitor my vital signs, I never felt more alone. My mother and father hadn't been to see me. Besides the police, doctors, and the average nurse, no one had.

I think my case manager back then explained the fact away with some spiel about reducing stimulus to help me adjust.

But I knew the truth they had been too polite to say: Leslie was dead. I wasn't. And while the townspeople may have crowed their relief to the local papers, few of them could look me in the eye.

Until he came, Heyworth Thorne. A pudgy, stout man with thinning brown hair, wearing a green suit that stretched at the middle. He stood tall despite the diminutive size, carrying himself like someone who mattered. Someone important.

Asked to consult on my case by the local police chief himself, he entered my hospital room with little more than a teddy bear and a strained smile. There was something rare tucked into the corners of his mouth though: genuine concern.

"Hello, Juliana," he said, dropping the crisp, polite tone everyone else used around me. His was blunter. Honest. "I know that nothing I could say would ever be good enough, or empathetic enough…" He cleared his throat and nodded to my empty bedside table. "So would you prefer we skip the introductions and I smuggle you some ice cream from the parlor down the street?"

The memory stings as I enter a different hospital room in the present day. God, I've always hated the crisp, antiseptic smell of the sterile environment. A chill seems to permeate the whole building—no different, no matter the state or year it's in, apparently.

The hushed, startled faces of everyone you pass are all the same: wide eyes, mouths contorted in pity. A hellscape of sympathy. Or perhaps an alternate reality serving as a gruesome juxtaposition to my memories.

My father is lying in my old place, tubes snaking from his body to feed various beeping machines. He looks so old. A frail stranger buried beneath white blankets.

"What happened?" I ask the room's only other occupant.

"Juliana." Diane, my stepmother, rises from a chair near the bed and swipes at her eyes with the sleeve of her cream sweater. "It started the other day. He didn't feel himself, enough that the doctor kept him overnight. Then this morning…" She shakes her head and buries her face in her hands. "Oh God, I don't know what we'll do if he doesn't…"

"I'll be in the hallway," Damien announces, releasing me as I step forward and throw my arms around Diane.

It's almost funny in a sense. I thought Simon and the horrors he put me through were the worst possible things I could face. I was wrong.

Seeing Heyworth, a man I spent more than half of my life admiring, lifeless cuts me to the core. I despise all the lies, the deception, and the pain he put me through.

But at the end of it all, he is still my father.

And I don't know if I can lose him for good.

R

"Juliana?" Someone taps my shoulder, their voice a whisper. "Go home, dear."

"H-Huh?" I startle upright and blink to bring my surroundings into focus: a plain white room with linoleum floors and a sterile view of the city beyond a wide window. Heyworth's hospital room. One glance at him, his eyes resolutely closed, and my body deflates. "I'm fine," I murmur, returning to the position I was sleeping in, with my face resting on my forearm. "I'm just resting for a second."

As my eyes drift shut, the person beside me sighs. Diane. "Sweetie, it's been two days."

I reopen my eyes and observe my body, contorted within an uncomfortable armchair. I'm still wearing my dress from Damien's studio. Two days. It's almost surreal, considering that in all that time—punctuated by a stream of doctors and nurses flooding in and out—my father's condition hasn't changed.

His prognosis is grim. They were able to destroy the worst of the clots in his brain, but each professional consulted on his case seems unsure of the long-term damage. If he wakes up at all, he might not be the same man.

It's so selfish to feel the way I do. Annoyed. As though he got the last laugh. I'll never learn the truth about him—or about Simon. But even as the thought unfurls, I cringe from it and reach for his hand, gripping it tight.

"I'm fine," I say, shrugging Diane off. "He could wake up any minute. I need to be here—"

"Juliana." She doesn't move. "You need to shower at least. And eat. And sleep. Think of what he would want? It certainly wouldn't be for you to jeopardize your own health, worrying about him. Besides"—she clears her throat and darts her gaze toward the door—"your friend may want some rest as well."

My friend?

Damien.

A familiar shadow is hovering near the doorway—the same spot I suspect he's periodically occupied during the past forty-eight hours. Not constantly, of course—but long enough.

I can't tell if Diane knows his identity or just doesn't care. Her pained expression is fixated solely on me.

"Please, darling." She cups my cheek against her palm, her blue eyes watering, her blond hair damp. She must have left and showered while I was sleeping, only to return wearing a fresh sweater and slacks. "I'll take over from here."

"Okay…" I've barely voiced the surrender when she takes my hand and helps me stand. Then she all but drags me to the door.

"I'll call you with any updates. I think you should take the day for yourself. Rest."

Rest. But how?

"No." I start to turn back. "I need to be here. I need to—"

"I believe you have been exiled." A firm hand captures mine before I can take another step, and its owner tugs me farther into the hall.

"But—"

"*Dulce niña.*" Lips tinged with the hint of cologne brush my earlobe. "I'll bring you back later. But I encourage you to take her advice."

God, I can only imagine how I look to have warranted the raw concern in his voice. How I must smell.

Surprisingly, Damien himself may give me an idea. Haggard. Even his blindfold can't disguise the full extent of his exhaustion. Shadows paint the hollows and contours of his jawline, making his age more apparent than ever. Stray strands have escaped from his usually slick ponytail. Unfairly, the lack of polish only adds to his intrigue. A passing nurse can't seem to take her eyes off him. At least until she glances at me and then shakes her head in pity.

"Come." His arm slips around my shoulders—a surprisingly intimate gesture. I stiffen until I realize why he's chosen this method: He can guide me without his cane. "Julio, if you please."

"*Sí.*" His guard appears as if conjured from the shadows. "This way, sir."

Damien herds me along after him, presumably tracking the sound of his footsteps. Far too soon, he's easing me into the back of his car, claiming the seat beside me.

"I need to make sure the nurses have my direct number," I say, toying with the idea of returning to the building. "What if—"

"You need to care for yourself," he insists. As if to demonstrate, he leans over me, finds my seat belt through feel, and fastens it over me. "You can return later. I will see to it. Julio, *vamanos*, if you please."

Given the sparse amount of vehicles surrounding us, we must be in a private section of the hospital's parking garage. As the car exits the structure, reality makes its presence painfully known. Hordes of reporters from various news outlets are camped on the outskirts of the property. Like vultures, they stand at the ready, waiting for a carcass to pounce on.

"They're here for me, aren't they?" I blurt.

"I've increased your security measures," Damien says without answering the question. "What happened the other day will not happen again."

"I...I need to go home." The hitch in my voice must betray exactly what I mean—*home*—because he nods and utters something in Spanish to Julio.

Minutes later, the car pulls up not in front of the Lariat, but my father's beautiful mansion in the hills. The reporters have made their way out here as well, clamoring near the front gate. Julio fearlessly navigates the spectators to the security checkpoint. One look at me and we're allowed through.

"I just need a minute," I tell Damien before slipping free of my seat belt and escaping the car altogether.

The front door opens when I turn the handle, but I'm not ready for the scent that hits me like a punch: Daddy's cologne.

His aftershave.

His old, comforting identity before lies revealed him as a stranger.

Tears flood my eyes and escape down my cheeks. I can't stop them, so I move instead, navigating the front hall until I reach his office.

Someone's been in here recently—or perhaps no one's touched it since my father last entered. God, his scent floods every ounce of space. I imagine him sitting at the desk, rummaging through his documents, plotting his triumphant return to politics. So concerned with appearances.

He couldn't even tell me that he'd blown off our meeting due to his health. Why? Did he think I'd accuse him of lying?

Maybe I would have.

Or maybe I'm the reason he's in the hospital in the first damn place. Did guilt exacerbate the blood clot? Guilt for lying to me…

Or fear? His perfect little doll might run away from his dollhouse forever. He's been keeping tabs on me, or so I infer from the newspaper clippings strewn all over his desk. Every single headline features my name, dating back weeks ago.

Juliana Thorne Takes Leave of Absence Amid Father's Scandal.

Juliana Thorne Linked Publicly with Family in Father's Botch Judgment.

Juliana Thorne, Rescued by a Hero: An Adoption Story.

Blinking frantically, I approach his coveted trophy case, displaying all of his awards. Heyworth Thorne, the golden citizen. Heyworth Thorne, a man who knew the identity of a monster and shielded him for over twenty years.

Heyworth Thorne, the very worst monster of them all.

My hands shake as I wrench the cabinet open and grab the first award I can reach: one for exemplar contributions to the city, shaped like a shooting star. Whirling on my heel, I throw it as hard as I can, narrowly missing a framed diploma hanging on the wall. As my vision blurs, I grab another. Another. They crash like missiles into various objects, knocking books from his shelves or careening into prized knickknacks. Was every bit of metal and glass worth more to him than I was?

They don't seem to matter so damn much now.

Panting, I yank the drawers out of his desk. The one near the bottom is already open and the edge of a folder is sticking out of it, as if shoved there, the last thing he may have read. His precious, coveted donor list? I grab it and callously scan the familiar, small handwriting scribbled on the front: *For Juliana.*

My body goes cold. As if from miles away, I hear a thud, and when I regain focus, I'm on my knees, hunched over the slim stack of documents. They're faded and dog-eared, delicate with age. Oh God… I recognize the crisp, cold layout of the topmost one as that of a police case file. Across the header reads *Juliana Mirangas, age 8.*

Numb, I scan each line, discovering nothing new. It's merely a summary of my statement and the events described. But the last page…

I've never seen it before: a different briefing referring to another case. Yet, in some ways, the events described are chillingly similar. The girl's name may be different, but the scattered bits of her statement resonate within me down to the bone.

"Wanted to play a game." "Didn't see a face." "Simon says…"

The date is a full year before my case, but unlike mine, a single suspect was questioned in this horrific crime. His name, however? It's been blacked out entirely. Even when I flip the page over and hold it up to the light, I can't read the letters marked over with black ink.

"Damn it!" I throw the file and watch the pages slowly drift down.

Even now, Heyworth refuses to divulge the answers I need. Answers only he can give.

Though no. He's not the only one. I flick through the pages for the older case file. The name of the girl… I read it over and over until it's cemented into my brain.

Lynn McKelvy.

Scrambling upright, I snatch up the remaining pages and carefully return them to their file, but when I reach an unfamiliar series of paragraphs, I freeze. *Psychiatric evaluation* screams across the top of the document, and the person described within the lines of text I know all too well.

__Juliana Mirangas__, age 8, female. School records convey poor attendance, average grades. Described as withdrawn and isolative by teachers. A fellow student referred to JM as "weird. Leslie was her only friend I think." No outward signs of prior trauma or psychiatric history. Family psych history of depression in mother. Father alcoholic with repeated parole violations stemming from an assault charge. Upon assessment with this writer, JM presented with a flat affect and mood and was evasive when asked about 10/28. Reports poor sleep, night terrors, anxiety. Current guardian reports that JM is fearful, guarded, and prone to emotional outbursts. Final impression: post-traumatic stress disorder, rule-out psychotic features.

Fearful, guarded, and prone to emotional outbursts. No wonder Heyworth watched over me so closely, tightening the leash whenever he felt I could threaten his precious political chances.

To him, I was always the same stray mutt: a damaged little girl with undiagnosed psychological issues. A threat to his reputation if left unchecked. A trophy to display for his benefit.

A toy to manipulate.

He never loved me.

He merely possessed me.

FIVE

amien is standing outside the car when I finally escape the house, battered file in tow. His clenched jaw betrays an unusual amount of concern. I wonder if he heard the chaos from here. Breaking glass. Broken trophies. A broken soul.

"You need rest," he rasps as I come closer. The authority in his tone warns that I won't be able to dissuade him this time. "I'm taking you to my—"

"Do you want to know what I really want?" I laugh. It's a trick question, no one ever does.

But he...

Damien goes silent, his head cocked. When he extends one of his hands toward me, I take it, surprised by how damn warm he feels. How much I crave that warmth. I'm freezing.

"Tell me," he demands.

"I want…" The sob I can't swallow has him pulling me closer. Too close. More tears spill into his jacket. Within seconds, I'm howling and nothing can keep the gasping cries from coming.

What do I want?

"Control," I wail brokenly. "I want… I just want answers! I'm so sick of being coddled, and watched, and whispered about. Did you know he put more effort into stalking my tabloid mentions than actually talking to me? I want to give them something to stare at! I'm so—"

"I know." His words undercut my high-pitched whine, low and steady. So damn assured. He knows. All of me. More than I care to admit to myself or name out loud. "I know, sweet girl. *Dulce niña.*" His fingers sink into my hair, finding my scalp. "And I'll give it to you. But first…" He pivots, guiding me toward the open door to the back seat. "You need rest. I won't take no for an answer, so don't resist just this once. *¿Sí?*"

Despite my pathetic little pleas, I nod. "Okay."

I let him control me.

Just this once.

Contrary to Damien's wishes, I can't sleep in spite of the exquisite quality of the bed and its luxurious sheets. I toss and turn for hours before eventually crawling off the mattress in defeat. I manage to shower at least, and I call Diane shortly before midnight.

"No change," she tiredly conveys. "And if you went by the house…"

"I'm sorry." I clench the fingers of my free hand, wincing as the nails dig into my palm. "I just—"

"It's okay," she says over me. "Don't worry about the damage. I've taken care of it. Just get some sleep, darling."

But I'm not tired.

I'm too damn hollow.

I hear him first, rounding the hallway beyond my room. His assured, slow steps betray just how well he has the layout memorized, though I doubt he's the type to intrude upon a sleeping woman without an invitation. No, I bet he heard me first, aware of me as much as I am of him.

When I turn to watch him appear in the doorway, the mug of steaming liquid in his hand confirms it.

Wordlessly, I approach him and accept the beverage offering: coffee, made to my preference. It's a gesture that conveys more than kindness: it's an acknowledgment of the obvious. I need to be awake.

"You brought these with you," he says, revealing something slender clutched in his other hand: the file from Heyworth's office.

"I'm sure you had Julio read them to you," I blurt—but I didn't intend to sound so hostile. "Thank you," I add, trying again. "But it's just trash. In fact, I should throw it away."

I reach for the file.

He doesn't extend it. "Trash," he murmurs, deceptively soft. With barely concealed interest, his fingers stroke the worn pages poking beyond the edges of the folder. "Your past. The truth you seek. The answers he hid from you. You call that trash? No, I don't think so."

Suddenly drained, I sip from the coffee and wander to the mattress, slumping onto the very edge. "That's not what I mean. I…" A watery giggle serves as the herald for the torrent of words I can no longer hold back. "Is it funny that I'd forgotten most of it? The details, I mean." Never Simon himself. "In some ways, I think I repressed it. Can you believe I forgot what my old name was? My real name: Juliana *Mirangas*." Another hollow laugh helps keep the tears at bay—for now. "At least that blows the whole 'Heyworth Thorne is racist' question out of the water. My mother had Spanish ancestry. Though, hell, maybe he is a fucking bigot and that made it easier for him to use me at all."

"Did you learn anything about your case?" Damien wonders. "Anything you might have forgotten?"

"No…" I shake my head. "But there is something I never questioned before. The local police chief back then asked my father—Heyworth Thorne—to consult on my case personally. But he was a defense attorney." I frown. It sounds even more unusual out loud. "Why would he ask a defense attorney to consult on a murder case?"

"Let alone one who practiced in a different state and jurisdiction?" Damien adds, stroking his chin. "Interesting. I intend to find out. I may have a contact at the city police department who may be able to help—though their chief is a man I don't particularly enjoy interacting with."

I raise an eyebrow. "Don't tell me. He's not a friend of yours? Not even after you insinuated blackmail to keep his men quiet about your sex club?"

"I would suggest you not extend your pity to Chief Harrison," he warns. "Trust me on that. Some men aren't nearly as righteous as they appear to the public."

"It takes one to know one, I suppose," I say.

"Perhaps," he admits. "But I will extend any resources I can to assist your search for information, whether or not they involve Harrison."

"There was something else," I murmur, running my hand through my hair as if to help shake the thoughts free. "In the file, there was information about another girl. Lynn McKelvy. Her case was similar to mine. She was attacked by a stranger, a man who had a knife and wanted to play a game of Simon Says..." I shudder, closing my eyes against the memories that threaten to descend. When I open them again, Damien is still here. "Can you help me find her? Maybe she knows something."

"Done," he says without hesitation either way. "But now we focus on you. You're upset—and I'm not just referring to what happened today. What can I do?"

I blink, overwhelmed by the genuine concern in his voice. The only way to smother the confusion is to drink more coffee, inhaling every drop until I've drained it all. Sighing, I shrug. "Make my father wake up and force him to tell me the truth?"

"If only I could." He laughs, but it's muted compared to his usual rich chuckle.

And I hate the fact that he's on edge around me. Wariness doesn't suit a man like him the way it does my father. Heyworth merely pretended to care; I see that now. But Damien?

He's too damn calculating to put on such an act. So what is his aim?

Watching him, I can't tell—and I do so for so long that my mug feels cool to the touch when I startle back to awareness.

"What can you do?" I whisper, recalling his question. "You taunted me once for being sheltered," I remind him. "Pathetic. Weak. A prude."

Not his exact words but close enough. The point was all the same.

"My father kept tabs on me," I admit. "Every fucking mention of my name, he collected from the tabloids, obsessing over them. My every move is cemented in ink, but that woman? She feels like a stranger. I..."

I stand and take a tentative step in his direction. My tongue flits along my lower lip as I process just how twisted my reality has become in only a few short days.

My father is lying in a hospital bed. He may be dying.

Yet I'm in the lair of Damien Villa, and for some reason, he seems to be the one damn person unwilling to treat me like a goddamn idiot. So what does a sheltered heiress do with her dangerous, masculine lifeline?

Test the hell out of him.

"Do you remember what you told me about the women at your club?" I ask. "That they have all the power?"

"*Sí*, I remember." He frowns and I can almost see him wrestling with the idea of humoring me or not. Indulgence must win, the cause of the slow smile that shapes his mouth. "Those women... In their hands, the obsessive attention of others is a weapon. They hone it sharp to their advantage. But few are brave enough to wield the same amount of control." His heated tone sends my blood racing. It's like he's invaded my mind again, goading me to voice my naughty desire out loud and in the open. "If you are curious, Ms. Thorne, I will ask you to admit as much *por favor*."

Holding my head high, I try. "So tell me, Mr. Villa. How... how does one feel in control like that?" My cheeks catch fire. I'm cringing at the raw vulnerability exposed by such a question.

Until his mouth quirks, a lethal smile. "I will tell you, sweet girl," he swears. "*But* I am not sure if I should. Sharing experiences is not one of my strong suits. From an entirely selfish standpoint…I should dissuade you."

God, the way he said that word. *Selfish*. It contained way more than possession—a grit making every syllable harder than it should be. I should be terrified. In fact, I am, according to the pitching sensation jolting my stomach. Terrified. Intrigued. Curious.

And in this moment, I can no longer beat around the bush.

"Make me forget, Damien," I say. I beg. "I need to forget. I need to…" My fingers tear through my hair, ripping at stray strands. "The reporters are everywhere I look. I can't even hate my father despite all he's done to me. I feel like I'm going insane—"

"*Sí.*" He's close before I realize it. Like liquid fire, his fingers find my chin, tilting it so our mouths are within dangerous reach. To heighten the nearness, his breath fans mine, searing and potent. "I will give you a taste of control. But I need you to promise me one thing."

I suck in a breath. "What?"

"That you will trust me."

Trust. That word takes on an entirely new connotation coming from him. It's more than a mere surrender of doubt —it's a surrender of sanity.

Of instinct.

Of safety.

To trust him will mean forsaking the one thing I've just begged him for.

I'll lose any shred of control.

I'll lose my goddamn mind.

"Can you do that for me?" His thumb traces the line of my jaw in a distracting, teasing swipe. "Give me your trust?"

"It's not like I have much of a choice," I admit in a whisper.

It's either him…

Or the horrors in my head.

With only a second to decide, I nod. "Yes."

"Good." His resigned frown takes my breath away. Like he said, he's breaking his own rules. For me. "Then get dressed. I will make the arrangements."

I watch him go, my nerves in knots. When I finally remember how to move, I start in the direction I assume the closet to be, trying to decide what one wears to regain control. Halfway across the room, I remember I'm not home.

"If you need something to wear, feel free to check the wardrobe. There is some clothing," Damien calls from down the hall as if realizing my dilemma. "You are welcome to wear whatever you like. I made sure to cater to your specific tastes."

Only he can make generosity seem like the most unsettling of threats.

Wary, I creep to a set of closed double doors and open them to reveal a luxurious walk-in closet. *Some clothing,* he said. More like a complete wardrobe, stocked with everything from shoes to items of jewelry displayed in a glass case. How thoughtful. How…prepared.

Flattery feeds a swarm of butterflies in my stomach until I recall his past muses.

Oh. No wonder he has a full boutique in house, given his proclivities.

Eyes narrowed, I flick through the items dangling from hangers and realize that they are all in my size. Every last item. Some are dresses in varying shades of crimson and navy. Some are simple blouses and slacks.

None are my customary bulletproof black.

I imagine him chuckling over that fact. Gloating. Any other day, I'd march toward him and deliver some haughty, scathing remark to prove how unaffected I am. Tonight, I bite back my pride and settle on a rich blue dress with a modest neckline and a knee-length hem. While outside of my usual wheelhouse of couture black, it's beautiful. The A-line shape hugs the contours of my body without feeling too restricting or revealing.

A fitting suit of armor to face an opponent like Damien Villa in. *Touché.*

He's in the foyer when I finally leave my room wearing my own pair of heels, clutching my purse to my chest. "So where are we going?" I muster up the courage to ask. "To your club?"

"I'm afraid not." He cocks his head in that predatory, hawklike way, and I swallow whatever else I meant to say. "Learning to take control is a methodical process, sweet girl. The first step is to cede it."

"I think I've been doing that my whole life. Ceding control," I add. God, I sound so petulant. "Letting everyone else manipulate me at every turn. I doubt you follow that step yourself."

"I do." He grabs my arm, pulling me closer before I can react. Soft and gentle, his fingers slide down my wrist and capture mine with a knowledge I will never get over. "When it matters," he insists, tightening his grip. "When a brief moment of control can tip the scales in favor of someone who needs that security. I can cede it, even despite my…preferences."

"Oh." My heart races, throat thickens. He's too close. His voice is too damn deep. Too earnest.

"However," he warns. "This will not work if you do not trust me."

"I-I can. I mean…I do."

"Good." He turns, guiding me to the door. "Then let us begin *por favor*."

Unsurprisingly, Julio is waiting in the hall to lead the way to the lower level. Given his appearance, I assume our destination is outside to a waiting car. Instead, we turn down a different hallway that leads deeper into the building. Eventually, we enter an elegant dining room, so out of place that it could have been conjured from thin air. Dark walls and wooden floors create an ebony backdrop for the round table draped in a pure white tablecloth, adorned with golden utensils.

In a way, it's a more terrifying battlefield than lying naked in front of a horde of strangers.

"Dinner?" I say thickly. "An interesting lesson, Mr. Villa."

"Patience," he replies, his upper lip quirked. With his free hand, he finds the back of one of the two chairs at the table and angles it toward me. "Yet another step that must be taken."

"And then?" I ask as I sit and watch him navigate his way to the chair opposite me. "Tell me: Is food the gateway drug to control?"

"No," he admits once seated. "But *knowledge* is. And to ensure your safety and comfort during our…arrangement, I need to know as much about you as you are willing to share."

"Oh?" I jut my chin haughtily into the air. "I thought there wasn't anything about me worth learning?"

His stern frown stubbornly remains. He wasn't joking. "I can admit when I have miscalculated. In your case, perhaps I have—enough to realize that, with you, I may have to adjust my own boundaries. So allow me to rectify that. I need to know your limits. What you are comfortable with. What you will not allow. And…" He pauses and an uneasy realization worms into my mind. He's hesitating.

"And what?"

"I need to know if you have any lingering trauma that may make our arrangement…unpleasant for you."

Ah, as polite a way of beating around the bush as I've heard.

"If you're asking if I was sexually assaulted, I wasn't," I say softly. "As far as monsters go, Simon was a different breed. He wasn't interested in my body, I don't think. Just my psyche. My sanity. My soul. But as far as the psychological trauma scale goes, we can check off daddy issues, trust issues, and post-traumatic stress disorder."

Is he relieved by that information? I can't tell. He sits like stone, his head tilted toward me, conveying that I have his full attention.

And yet…

I can't shake the sense that he's hiding something. Or perhaps avoiding.

"You're uncomfortable with the notion of sex," he points out. "Though not sexuality. You seem to have no problem relishing in your mastery on that front."

My cheeks burn as I remember all of the many ways he's gotten to experience me relishing in said sexuality.

"In fact, if I may be so bold…"

I swallow hard and scan the table in search of wine. There is none. I have to fight this battle of wits with no armor to hide behind.

"Yes?" I croak when the passing seconds make it clear that he needs an answer. "You can be bold."

"I'm curious if you are partial to exhibition."

I nearly choke. By the grace of God, I spit out a reply instead. "Like what takes place at your little club?"

"Yes." He nods. "Like what takes place at my little club. Women, comfortable in their sex, empowered enough to bare it all for the rich, closeted clients willing to pay through the teeth to watch. It's the clients who pretend as though they have the upper hand—the dignity in the situation, you see—but no." He scoffs, shaking his head. "The woman they sneer down at. Scorn. Ogle. She knows who has the real power. They all wish they could be so free."

"Free…" I eye the elegant, polished table setting and flick my thumb along the edge of a silver fork. "And if I *was* into exhibition?"

I don't dare look at his face, but the sound he makes… Part startled grunt, part amused laugh. I squirrel it away in some far recess of my brain to parse over later.

"In some ways, I wouldn't be surprised," he admits, startling me. "A woman such as yourself, always in the public eye, always watched and whispered about. How did you put it? *'I want to give them something to stare at.'*"

"So fine, you got me. I want to writhe naked in front of a bunch of strangers." How I said that without laughing, I will never understand. "But *you* don't. You strike me as a private man, Mr. Villa. One who doesn't enjoy sharing his experiences."

"There are ways to satisfy both of our requirements," he says softly. "If that is what you desire."

"How so?" I ask instead. "You throw me to the wolves, letting your male 'entertainers' screw me while you sit back and watch?"

What I intended as a joke lands more like a grenade.

"No." He sits straighter, and were his eyes whole, I'd imagine them flashing. "I apologize if I was not clear before. No one will ever touch you but me." His voice is so thick that I feel it in my fucking bones. Crackling tension robs every ounce of air from my lungs—but a second later, his posture relaxes and I can breathe again. "At least until our arrangement is over. *Sí*, that is one boundary of mine I will never bend."

"So how—"

"I need to know if this is truly what you want. You need to be sure, no doubts or second-guessing. Once I finalize the arrangements, there is no going back."

Even considering what he's offering should be ludicrous. One might argue it could easily be written off as driven by extreme emotional distress, at the very least. Deep down, I know it's not. I have no excuse of mental frailty to fall back on. The same impulse driving me now is the same one that drew me to his art in the first place, I suppose.

Curiosity. Discontentment. Enthrallment. Jealousy.

"*Dulce niña*, how about I tell you?" he murmurs before I can reply. "You may correct me if I am wrong, *¿sí?* But as much as you may try to deny it, you want to be like them. You want to know what it's like to be on fucking display— but on your own terms for once. You want—no, need—to let the world see you as you are, in a way they can't mock or deride or scrutinize. It's why you wanted me to paint you in the first place, is it not? This desire you feel… It is more than lying naked on a pedestal on a rebellious whim— because you've already stripped yourself bare, robbing them of any ammunition to use against you."

His words reflect an assessment that goes far beyond this moment. He's amassing everything he learned during his unknown months of surveilling me.

"There is a hesitation in you," he adds as if to prove as much. "A fear I doubt you are even aware of. Something that makes you unafraid to bare your skin yet causes you to flinch when I touch you, even as you moan. I believe it is deeply rooted in why you've remained alone for so long. One of the reasons I asked for your trust was in the hopes that we can both learn what is really troubling you."

Something more than the past, he seems to imply.

"We can discuss it further after you eat," he adds, gesturing to the doorway.

A waiter appears as if on cue, carrying the caliber of fare I've come to expect from a man with his taste: an entrée of expertly seared steak on a bed of fresh greens paired with a serving of wine to wash it all down.

I sample everything, tasting nothing. Eventually, I find myself watching Damien more than anything else. He manipulates a fork and a knife, mechanically chewing every now and again, but I'm not fooled by his air of indifference. I sense that his full attention is on me. Listening to every scrape of my utensils over my plate, tracking how much I consume.

He's studying me, compiling a dossier of my behavior that I bet contains far more secrets than the one I discovered in my father's office.

"All right." Sighing, I finally set my fork aside. "So, what if I lied before?" I try my damn hardest to sound nonchalant. Like these words don't matter—when, in reality, they symbolize everything. "About why I'm still a virgin. What if Simon *does* have everything to do with it?"

"*¿Sí?*" He copies me and carefully dabs at his mouth with the tip of an ivory napkin. "Then I would be assured that my skills of deduction haven't drastically degraded within the span of twenty-four hours," he says. "Tell me the truth *por favor*."

"It's childish," I admit. "But…I've never stopped seeing his shadow everywhere I look. And I've always thought, even though I know it's ridiculous…" Tears sting my eyes and I frantically blink them back. "I-I can't stop…"

"Go on," Damien encourages.

"I've always felt that if I let anyone else in… One day, they'll leave and it may prove him right. All along, I wasn't worth it. Leslie should have lived, not me." I choke out a watery laugh, but I know even he can sense the tears I can't keep from falling. "My virginity, as stupid as it sounds, was one of the few fucking things that was always *mine.* No one else's. My parents, my innocence, my friend—I've lost everything else. I can't lose any more. Not to him."

"I'm sorry." Damien pushes back from the table. "Perhaps I did miscalculate. I am not the man you should surrender such trust to—"

"But you're wrong."

He stiffens and slowly lowers himself onto the chair.

"Is it pathetic that you're one of the few people in my life to *ask* me who I am? What I want? I don't think you understand how much that affects me," I concede. "Being asked a question and having someone actually care about the answer. If you're worried about hurting me, then don't be. Love isn't what I need from people. I've had it. Have it. I know I could easily find someone out there to cherish me. A man who would coddle me and keep me on a leash just like Heyworth has. But it's not what I want. Not what I need. I need…challenge. Someone who will shove me into a room stocked only with blank canvas and dare me to strip."

His jaw twitches as though he's recalling that very memory.

"A man who tests my limits and preys on my fears," I continue. "I'm sorry if this is making you uncomfortable—"

"No. Never." He shakes his head. "Far from it. But I am not sure if I am quite the man you think I am. I could disappoint you."

"And I think that's part of the thrill," I confess. "You could. You could be the worst kind of monster under all this suave polish. But for some reason, I still want to play your twisted little game a little longer."

Unlike Simon, at least he's given me a choice.

"So, now what?" I ask, pushing my plate aside. "More stalling?"

"Oh, no, Ms. Thorne." His devilish laugh stiffens every hair on the back of my neck. "Now, I'll take you up on your proposal. We will play my twisted game. May the best man win."

"Or woman."

"*Sí, sí.*" He chuckles even more deeply. "Or woman."

SIX

We arrive at his club well past the hour when other establishments would be closing. I vaguely recognize the gilded hallway marking his private entrance, but this time, we stop short of the hall leading toward the viewing booths.

There's a peculiar tension I sense in the air even before he speaks.

"I'll allow you a minute to rethink your request," he warns, his hand on mine, imparting heat. "You say the word and we'll leave. I'll take you home and you can rest—because I'm partly sure delirium may be fueling your newfound lust to experience the forbidden."

I have to laugh at that. "No," I say, shaking my head—for my own benefit, not his. "I…I'll play your game, Mr. Villa. I *want* to."

"Then play you shall." He lowers his mouth near my ear. "You will star alone tonight," he says, dropping all pretense. No more word games. This is real. "Just you in front of a full audience—but I want you blindfolded. I'll let you wonder as to their faces. Their identities. Their reactions. Because none of them matter to you, do you understand? This performance is for *me*. Show me who the sheltered girl is behind her mask. Reveal to me what she needs. In a sea of these pretentious fucking people, you listen for *me*."

He draws back as his words ripple down my spine.

"Daphne will assist you from here," he calls to me while advancing toward the viewing rooms. "I look forward to your performance, Ms. Thorne. I do suggest that you follow *all* of her instructions. *Adios*."

"Hello." Daphne is a smiling blond in a slimming black dress who appears as if conjured. "Follow me, Ms. Thorne," she says before heading in the direction opposite Damien. "Mr. Villa has made all of the arrangements."

I don't know what I expect to discover when she finally ushers me into a small room. An elegant vanity and a wooden wardrobe would be far down on my list. It's an intimate, surprisingly tasteful setting adorned with a ruby color scheme similar to the theater-like atrium I viewed the last time he brought me here.

"You can undress," Daphne says. Then she crosses the room and points out a door opposite from the one we entered through. "You can leave through here when you are ready," she explains. "It opens to the stage."

"Is that where…where I'll be blindfolded?" I ask.

Daphne shakes her head. "No. Once you are ready, I'll be waiting on the other side." She nods to the door again.

"There, I'll blindfold you as well as relay Mr. Villa's final instructions. There is a robe you can put on until then," she adds as if sensing the nerves crawling up my throat, robbing me of my voice. "Whenever you are ready."

She slips through the door, leaving me alone, and I eye my reflection in the vanity's mirror.

I look so young. So tired. Purplish bruises encircle my eyes, and my ratty hair is in dire need of a deep condition and a brush.

No wonder Damien changed his mind so suddenly on indulging my impulsive request. As I look now, few men would desire me.

Once I strip my coat, my beautiful dress enhances my appearance, but only by a little. I'm a dull, plain shadow overall. The kind of woman who may be whispered about and hounded but only because she makes for such an easy target.

A haunted, hollow doll.

My fingers shake as I reach around to my back, searching for the zipper of the dress. When it's loosened, the fabric easily falls, revealing more pale, unremarkable skin.

In a horrible way, I'm relieved Damien is blind. He can't see the gaunt, rail-thin body I do. Or the scars on my thigh. Or the fear in my eyes.

Yet he somehow sees beyond it all, peering beneath the flesh to the parts of me I can't disguise. Now, I think I know exactly why he changed his mind; this is a test, designed for me more so than him.

Can I truly trust him despite all the people who may be watching? Whispering? Judging?

Am I that fragile doll Heyworth coddled or an opponent worthy of playing the monster's game?

The answer terrifies me as I step out of my shoes and approach the closed door, knocking once.

I don't know.

But I want to find out.

*D*aphne stays true to her promise. At my knocking, she opens the door, a slender strip of black silk dangling from her opposite hand. Without a word, I turn, allowing her to secure the blindfold over my eyes. It's soft against my skin but impenetrable—a sheet of endless dark.

"There is one more thing Mr. Villa insisted upon," she murmurs.

I jump as a cold, hard surface brushes my ear and settles against the lobe. Solid. Slightly heavy. My thoughts spin, desperately trying to put a name to the object.

"This way," Daphne says without giving an explanation herself.

Taking my hand, she leads me forward and I can almost feel the atmosphere shift from the stale, close air of the hall to the wider, echoing theater. My first thought is to assume it's empty—Damien Villa wouldn't dare share his new doll with the world.

He's merely toying with me.

But faint murmurs and whispers nibble at my ears to spite my pathetic assumption. People—more than one.

"You can lie here," Daphne suggests, stopping short.

I tentatively reach out, alarmed as my fingers brush a silken surface that gives slightly when I apply pressure. A mattress? I lower myself onto it, and soft footsteps betray Daphne's retreat. Barring the audience, I'm alone in this arena now. Thin fabric forms a fragile base beneath me as unseen eyes take in more of me than anyone has ever seen. The blindfold obscuring my vision serves as my lone piece of armor.

And I don't even know how many spectators are present. Ten? Twenty? Hundreds? Their murmured voices echo in a constant hum: an ocean of rejection, or scrutiny, or judgment.

Panic sets in. My hands twitch upward to cover myself as my heart hammers a silent command against the inside of my rib cage: *run*.

I can't do this. I can't…

Wait. That low, rumbling clearing of a throat rises above all other noise. I'm insane—there's no way I could pick him out so easily. So definitively. It's another man I'm straining my ears to catch. A stranger, whose voice drips directly into by ear, fed by the object nestled there. An earpiece, I realize.

"Sweet *dulce niña.* Did you think I'd let you have full rein for your little performance?" His deep, raspy laugh twists my stomach into knots. "I warned you: This performance is for me."

"Oh?" I gasp, unsure if he can even hear me through the device.

But he can—another grated chuckle proves it, laced with faint hints of static.

"I thought you were supposed to be teaching me control?" I whisper—but even the faint sound isn't loud enough to drown out the persistent hints of the others in attendance. I can smell them. Perfume. Cologne. Cigar smoke. An amalgam of strangers watching me. Waiting.

They demand entertainment.

"This is mine," Damien declares as casually as if commenting on the color of the sky. "Lie back. Do not hide. Place your hand on your belly. Now breathe deeply. Like that."

I obey, letting the sound of my breathing and the blood humming through my veins drown out all other noise.

"Keep it there and let your other hand sweep along your hip. Feel the softness of your skin. Like silk, *¿sí?*"

I don't know if it's his voice or the warm sensation of my fingertips gliding over me that hypnotizes me. First my throat, then skimming down the sides of my breasts, across my stomach. Back up.

"Now…spread your legs, sweet girl. Let them see what they will never have."

I stiffen. Refusing is my first reaction. I almost can't bite it down. "I can't—"

"*Sí*," Damien growls. "You will. Nice and wide, sweet girl." God. A moan edges his voice so unexpected in that grated tone.

My body jerks, my thighs parting as if of their own accord.

"You've done it," he hisses as if spitting the words through clenched teeth. "I can hear them gasping. So beautiful. So pink—"

Heat floods my cheeks and I almost stop listening. Shut down. Ignore.

But he's right. I can hear a distinctive shift in the room: a change presented in a sudden hush the farther my legs drift apart.

"Touch yourself," Damien commands, his voice so damn thick. Each word is drenched in his accent, barely recognizable as English. "Just once. *Mierda*." He hisses as I slip my hand between my legs. "Good girl. I can hear your breathing change. Again *por favor.*"

My finger grazes a sensitive ball of nerves and a cry rips from my throat. Nerves prickle and twitch, unsure of how to process each hesitant touch. With pleasure? Shame? Both? My quivering thighs battle to close together. Hide. Retreat. God, who knows who could be watching. What they see. How I look.

And the more my brain runs through every frantic fear and scenario, the less they seem to matter.

"Stop," Damien snarls, jarring me back to the present. "I said *once*, sweet girl. I doubt these bastards deserve more —*mierda!*" he grunts as my finger slips, which draws another gasp from my lips. "You're disobeying, Juliana." A hoarseness laces the warning—he sounds anything but upset. "Don't stop there, then. Add another finger, sweet girl."

A part of me shies from the dare. But another, bolder impulse seizes control of my limbs. Two fingers stroke my flesh in tandem. It's lightning. My back arches, my throat contracting around another strangled cry.

"Imagine I'm there with you," Damien murmurs. "Remember what it was like when you were at my mercy."

I stiffen at the memory, the images almost too sinful to imagine—but my brain produces them anyway. Him kneeling in front of me. His heat on me. Inside…

"Yes," he grates. "You're touching yourself again. I can tell. I can practically taste you, even from here." He curses. "Stop. Too much—"

But I can't. Forsaking his order, I perform solely for me, letting my fingers twist and stroke of their own accord. Harder. Faster. Deeper.

"This is what I wanted for you," he growls heatedly. "Selfishness. Greed. They all want you, sweet girl. But you're mine, aren't you? Can you sense them?"

I can. They're staring. Focused only on the image I'm displaying. Only what I want them to see.

A million people may be in this room, but he's inside my head. Listening. Studying the slick sound of every stroke of my finger. Imagining himself touching me instead. I bet he can sense the moisture growing the longer this moment extends. The world may be watching, but none are sensing the same things he is. Smelling me with flared nostrils. Tasting me in the air.

I picture him interpreting every little sound I make, imagining their cause.

He wanted to know my limits. My wants. My desires.

Perhaps they're pathetically simple? I need him to see me— to explore me in a way no one else would dare. Deeper than any other man could. Harder and more intimately than anyone else has the right to.

I want him.

I want him.

I want him to want me just as insanely.

I'm on the verge of something soul-shatteringly destructive when I catch that low, tortured growl again. It's a promise, ringing true even as my sharp gasp drowns it out.

He'll give it to me, those dangerous things I desire.

Whether I'm ready or not.

SEVEN

Somehow, I manage to stand on jellied legs and return to the dressing room. Daphne helps me into my dress, but when I finally reenter the lobby, Julio is the one waiting for me. Damien is nowhere to be seen. Not even as we exit the building and enter the car idling out front.

He isn't in his suite, either. The stale air lacks his trademark scent as Julio ushers me inside while remaining in the hall. In fact, all I smell is my own sweat, and nervousness rises like a slap, erasing the thrill from the club.

As childish as it fucking sounds, did I do it wrong? Did I upset him somehow, even though I followed his damn instructions to the T? I listened for him. Performed for him. Bared myself to him.

And the bastard can't even pat me on the back for a job well done.

Damn it. I hate what uncertainty does to me when it comes to him. It nibbles, chewing at my nerves in a way disappointing Heyworth never did. Wearing a mask for my father was a superficial game—this one has gone deeper. Too deep.

My cheeks sear as I linger in the foyer, debating whether or not to even stay. Could I face him? Let him laugh: *Silly Juliana, it was all a game. You gave me plenty of fodder to sell to the tabloids, however. Gracias.*

I turn for the door and brace my hand on the doorknob—but I don't know what makes me release it in the end. Maybe pride. I won't give him the satisfaction of running this time. I'll meet him head-on. Because even if this was some cruel, sick form of humiliation…

I don't regret it.

The thought gives me the strength to march into my room, my head held high like the bastard's watching. Maybe he is —listening anyway. He can hear me laugh in defiance of his goddamn mind games. He can hear me…

Gasp as I leave the monotone color scheme of his suite and enter a world of roses. Beautiful, swollen budding roses in more colors than I have considered possible. Natural. They cover nearly every available surface, spilling from vases or in petals scattered over the bed and the floor. In the midst of it all is a silver box perched on one of the pillows. An ivory card lies beside it.

I pick up the card first with trembling fingers. All it contains is a slash of elegantly penned script: *You were exquisite.*

Not quite the reaction one would expect when paired with cold, disappearing silence.

Intrigued, I set the card aside and turn my attention to the silver box. It's thin, delicately crafted, and when I lift the lid to reveal what's inside it, it takes every muscle I possess to keep from dropping it.

Lying on a bed of red silk is a thin silver chain suspending a single perfectly round pearl.

And I know before I even run my finger along the edge of it that it's *the* pearl.

Our pearl.

I put it on, shivering as it settles between my breasts. So delicate…

And yet so dangerous.

So damning.

*A*fter everything I've been through, it should be impossible to sleep. Impossible. Yet I wind up blinking my eyes open to pale light flooding the room of Damien's suite. My nostrils flare, swollen with floral scents. Sighing, I roll onto my side and scan the room, observing the forest of roses in the different lighting—and they are still here.

But I'm sure I closed the door last night before stripping my clothing and climbing beneath the sheets. It's open now, and in the shadows of the hall, something draws me from the bed for a better look.

A potted arrangement blocks my path—one that I'm sure wasn't there last night. Carefully nestled in an ivory vase, an array of orchids and lilies in varying shades of white clamor for sunlight. So beautiful and—in a way—so wasteful.

Breathtaking gesture aside, it's a fact that all of these flowers will be dead within days.

As I finger the pearl hanging from my throat, I have to wonder if that's his point. Beauty decays. Natural freshness withers. A true artist would seek what he could from such fragility and then move on from the rotting husk. Does he look at me the same way? A beautiful bloom to be plucked at just the right moment. I'll make for a lovely diversion for a while, but eventually, he'll have to toss me aside and find another bud to corrupt.

It's the natural order of things.

Noise from the other room draws my attention and I rake my hands through my hair, clearing the morbid thoughts as I follow the hall.

I find Damien waiting for me in the living room of the penthouse, seated on the leather chaise. Damn. Despite his penchant for disappearing, the man can cut a figure when he wants to. An ebony suit enhances his broad shoulders and a blood-red tie creates a startling contrast of color.

My fingers twitch, still caressing his pearl. For a second, I consider creeping toward him, potentially catching him off guard. Perhaps I'd run my fingers along his skin, tracing the stern line of his jaw he hides so well around me. But the second I cross the threshold of the room, he stiffens.

"I apologize for last night."

"Huh?" I clear my throat to disguise my surprise. Odd. It's not quite what I was expecting: a genuine apology uttered in a guttural baritone. "Don't tell me, Mr. Villa," I start, feigning nonchalance as I linger in the doorway. "You didn't want an encore?"

"Far from it," he counters, shifting to face me.

Damn. My inner thighs clench as his tongue dances along his lower lip.

"I had to sleep in my studio in fact, to ensure I didn't insist on that very scenario."

My heart lurches in my chest. "Oh?"

"*Sí.* The intricacies of your little performances never cease to intrigue me," he admits, sounding even raspier. His hands are braced over his knees, the knuckles damn near white in comparison to the rest of his skin. "I can only imagine how much you enjoy thwarting my expectations at every turn."

He makes it sound criminal: thwarting him. Confusing him. Surprising him.

I suppose I should feel smug. Instead…

"Thank you," I croak, turning away as my cheeks heat. "I mean it. I…I didn't know how much I needed a diversion until—"

"I understand," he says, only unnerving me further. "But you did ask me for one other favor, and before we discuss last night, I owe it to you to report what I've found."

"Did you find her?" Hope bubbles up, distorting my voice before I can choke it back. "The other victim? Is she—"

"I did," he says carefully. "But it's bad news, I'm afraid. Lynn McKelvy died several years ago."

The stress he put on that terrible word sends my brain spinning with a million possible reasons. "How?"

"An overdose," he says.

"You mean she killed herself." I cross my arms over my chest—they're trembling. "Didn't she?"

His solemn nod is all the confirmation I need.

"That's awful." I stagger forward and wind up sitting beside him, my face pressed to my palm. My head is spinning. God, I can't think. The weight of everything comes bearing down, a torrent of conflicting emotions. Guilt. Pain. Rage.

"Awful," Damien agrees. "But what happened to her is not your fault—"

"Isn't it?" I counter bitterly. "All this pain and my father knew. How could someone be so selfish? How?"

Though I could ask myself the same question. I haven't looked at my cell phone since last night for a reason. Dread of what I might find? Fear of what I might not?

I don't even know if him being alive or dead terrifies me more.

"How could he lie to me?" The kind, lovely man who comforted me all those years ago. Who snuck candy into my hospital room. The doting yet stern figure who bought me a puppy for my ninth birthday and rented out the entire zoo for my enjoyment. No matter how hard I try, I can't reconcile that man with the monster all facts point to him being. "How could he—"

"If it is any consolation, there may be one way for you to find some ounce of closure." He slips a hand into the pocket of his coat and withdraws, of all things, a slim, pink book. Stickers coat the cover in a mockingly colorful collage given the morbid topic of conversation—and something tells me it's not his. It looks old and well worn, swollen with crinkled, written-on pages. "Lynn McKelvy kept a journal that her sister salvaged from her belongings. At my request, she's loaned it to me. Do you want it?"

I force my fingers to uncurl, gripping the end of it. Overall, it's barely the width of my palm, yet it feels so weighty in my grasp. Balanced on my lap, I don't know if it's a gift.

Or a curse.

"Thank you—"

"I would caution you not to. At least not yet." He stands, finding his cane. "But I hope it brings you some measure of comfort."

"Have you read it? I mean, had Julio read it to you?"

A muscle in his jaw lurches and I marvel at that. Not smugness for once. Unease? "No," he says.

"Why not?"

Men like him don't relinquish knowledge so easily. Lynn could have written about the menial ins and outs of her daily life—or Simon.

Yet he's given it to me first.

"Thank you."

"I have business I need to attend to," he says, heading for the door, his cane in hand. "I'll return later."

"I should go home anyway," I say, standing as well. "I appreciate you letting me stay here—"

"Oh, that is right. We never did clarify this one, small matter." He inclines his head, displaying that dangerously charming smile. "I will continue to uphold my end of our bargain, but in return, you fulfill one daily task for me, *¿sí?*"

A shiver runs down my spine as I force myself to reply. "Oh? Like what?" It's chilling how quickly he can turn the tables. I never know what to expect from one minute to the next. Charming Damien? Mocking Damien? Disarmingly gentle Damien?

"You sleep here for as long as this arrangement persists. Though I will remind you that you've already agreed to do so."

"W-What? But I—"

"I'll see you later tonight," he says, but this time, it sounds less reassuring. More like a dare. Or a threat.

"I suppose you'll pay for my things to be brought here?" I inquire, placing my hands on my hips. "I mean, your clothes are lovely, but I would prefer my own. If I'm to stay here for any period of time, at least."

There. I *almost* sound confident, but if he's caught off guard, his posture doesn't reveal it.

His back is to me as he continues his slow, lazy pace to the door—but his laugh resonates in my belly. "Of course. I'll make the necessary arrangements."

"And," I add, waiting until he pauses near the entrance to the foyer, "no listening devices. If I want you to hear me, you'll hear me. If not, you accept that." The seriousness in my tone negates the playful nonchalance I wish to convey. But it's like he said: He wants me to trust him.

And I can't if he treats me like an enemy one second and a plaything the next.

"I mean that," I insist as seconds pass without a response. "Please."

"As you wish. *Adios*." The door opens and his footsteps drift into the hall. "We will have dinner tonight," he adds before leaving entirely. "I'm afraid pizza, however, will not be on the menu."

In a telling display of leverage, he doesn't give me the chance to refuse before the door closes after him.

Touché.

Alone, I hunch into myself. I'm shaking, twisting that goddamn journal over and over until I finally gather up the nerve to open it. The first entry is dated over four years ago. In surprisingly neat script, Lynn McKelvy recorded her day-to-day thoughts. She had a boyfriend named Tim. A sister named Sarah. Wonderful, attentive parents.

And…she hated her birthday. Dreaded it in fact. That single looming date dominates nearly every passage. In the same sentence where she bemoaned boring chores or a shitty day at work, she prefaced it with a single foreboding statement: *It's a month until my birthday. A week. A day.*

Until the date finally came and went. Afterward, the entries become sparser. Less coherent. The last scribbled statements chill me to my core,

It didn't happen. No card. No present. He didn't come.

And I should be relieved…

But I'm not.

EIGHT

*L*ynn McKelvy feared her birthday—not the day itself, but what it meant. Midnight ushered in a series of disturbing events that had become a ritual of sorts. They seemed so benign on paper: receiving a card from an unwanted well-wisher. A few carefully curated presents, all from *him*.

A reminder of the hell she barely survived as a child.

But four years ago, in her case, they seemingly stopped coming.

And rather than relish that fact, it terrified her.

As I finish the last page of the journal, there's only one method I can think of to salvage what I can from the smoldering wreckage of my sanity.

Step one: ignore reality—starting with shoving Lynn McKelvy's diary beneath the pillow in my room and pretending it doesn't exist. It's foolish. Childish, but I'll worry about the consequences later.

Now, it seems far more vital to wallow in a scalding-hot shower and attempt to erase Damien Villa from my skin. Scrubbing and soap are no match; he stains my flesh like oil paint, highlighting the glaring flaws I'm used to suppressing. In the end, I scuttle into a robe in defeat.

My hollow gaze watches me from the mirror's surface, noticing the subtle ways he's tainted me. The skin on my neck flushes pink as if remembering his touch. Even the usual fear surging through my veins feels different now. Electric, capable of sowing more damage upon my psyche than a few memories.

Like those of my own hated birthdays.

Simon's never missed a single one. Those three tortuous days always play out in chilling predictability. First, the wine—merely a card when I was younger—followed by a wrapped newspaper clipping from the day I went missing, then the doll, a replica of Leslie's. Then a rose.

And finally…

I rack my brain for the image required to fill in the blank. Every single year, it came on the third day without fail, but this year…

Bile congeals into a creeping creature, crawling up my throat. *No…* I rake my fingers through my hair as if searching for that one terrible memory. But I can't find it. How ironic that over a week of chaos has allowed me to forget. *This* year, on the third day, my final present never came.

Logic escapes my brain as I throw my coat on and lunge for the front door of the suite, ripping it open. I hear someone call my name as I race to the elevator and ride it to the lower floor, but I can't stop. Panting, I tear onto the street and flag down the first cab I can, taking it straight to the Lariat.

"Hey!" the driver snaps as I shove the door open and climb out without bothering to hear the fare. "You owe me, lady!"

But he'll just have to get in line.

My once familiar, if cold home is a labyrinth now. A few nights away have warped the gilded hallways, transforming luxury into a foreboding maze. My front door is the portal to a nightmare world and every nerve urges me to run as I open the door and step inside.

On the surface, it looks as I left it last. No avalanche of flowers. No lurking Damien Villa.

No final, haunting warning from Simon.

Though perhaps he decided to deliver it in person?

A shadow flickers on the fringes of my entryway—near the kitchen. A stranger. A man. Panic paralyzes me. It takes a heart-stopping second before I notice the uniform the intruder is wearing, the navy blue of a police officer.

"Can I help you?" I blurt in a rush.

"Ms. Thorne," he says, stepping from behind my counters, his hands elevated. "Sorry to bother you, but Chief Harrison wanted me to secure—"

"Secure?" I croak. "Just because my father's in the hospital, that doesn't mean you get to do his bidding. Not without a warrant or whatever it is you need."

He raises an eyebrow. "Ma'am, I was sent by the chief. For your safety. Apparently, there's an investigation into—"

"I'm sorry." My chest heaves as those dangerous keywords land on the overwhelming pile on my psyche like drops of gasoline. "Just please g-get out!" I point a trembling finger toward the door. "Now! Get out!"

"Of course." The man lurches past me and respectfully inclines his head. "Sorry to startle you."

The full extent of just how badly he has doesn't sink in until the door finally closes after him. My knees tremble, knocking together. I have to stagger forward and brace my hands over the counter just to stay upright. My poor, abandoned pot of oleander wilts nearby: a few naked stalks amid a swath of fallen petals.

I brush my finger along the rim of the tiny pot, remembering its original intent: to terrify me. One morbid present accounted for—though not one of Simon's.

Pushing myself upright, I remove my coat before I leave the kitchen in search of my fourth gift.

And I rip the entire suite apart looking for it. His usual spot would be the bathroom, taped to the mirror, my final reminder of why we play his twisted game.

But it's not there.

Or in the hall.

Or in my bedroom.

I give up somewhere in the middle of searching the walk-in closet. Around me, I sense the world continuing, the day elongating. Shadows loom and deepen across the floor, but I can't move. It's selfish in retrospect. My father could be dying. Damien could be moving on to his next conquest.

Or Simon could be waiting to finish me off once and for all.

When heavy footsteps intrude into my suite, I'm convinced it's him—ha, not even a police presence would deter him. My old tormentor has come to finish me off for good. Is that what really happened to Lynn McKelvy?

I should feel terror building with every slow, approaching step.

But I don't.

All I can do is tilt my head to watch a figure appear in the threshold of my room, bathed in indigo twilight.

"I did offer to retrieve your things," Damien announces before advancing a step. "Though I will admit your method seems more…lively." He tentatively nudges a wad of clothing strewn across his path with his foot, but his clenched jaw betrays just how unsure he is. One of his hands feels out in front of him to maintain his balance, a rare sign of instability.

"Wait!" I lurch upright and kick any nearby objects out of his way. "I'm sorry, I—"

"You're crying." He grabs my wrist with uncanny insight, pulling me toward him. His cocked head warns that he's tracking every hitch in my voice. There's no point in trying to disguise it. "I know packing can be overwhelming for some, but I suspect that is not the case in this instance."

"Lynn McKelvy was attacked by Simon," I croak in a rush. "I know it was him. He haunted her on her birthday too. Every year. But then one year, he stopped…and she died—"

"Slow down," Damien urges. His hand sinks into my hair, parting the thick strands. Subtly applied pressure urges me closer to him until my face is resting against his chest. "Breathe."

"She died," I stammer, fisting my hands in the front of his coat. "And I don't—what if he killed her? What if he's planning to finally kill me? My last present never came." Tears stream down my cheeks, heedless of the fingers I deploy to combat them.

"Easy. Easy, sweet, girl." Damien shifts, fully engulfing me in his arms. "Talk to me."

"It never came," I insist, between gasping sobs. "He always sends it on the third day, always."

"What?" he demands, but his voice is tenser. Brittle. "Talk to me, sweet girl. What didn't come?"

"A picture," I confess. I can see it: the same sick image used to torment me every single year since I was eight years old. Squeezing my eyes shut doesn't erase it. "My class picture from second grade."

Scrawled across it would be the same mocking phrase, year after year: *Was she worth it?*

Was my life worth Leslie's?

The answer resonates in my soul, just as true now as it was then: *No.*

"What if he kills me too? What if…what if he hurt my father?" I can't even imagine the prospect, and my fingers tighten over the luxurious fabric in their grasp. "People connected to your brother's case have wound up dead lately. What if—"

"No one will harm you," Damien says as though it's as solid a fact as the sky being blue. We breathe air. He'll protect me. "Though I can't say the same for myself…" His pained tone draws my attention down to my hands. I'm clutching his arms, nails drawn.

"S-Sorry!" I loosen my grip, but he captures my hand before I can pull away completely.

"You don't ever need to apologize to me."

"Not even for suspecting you of the unthinkable?" I counter. "I can't lie and say I haven't considered it, that you could be the reason my father is in the hospital. What if you wanted to hurt him that badly?"

He's gone as far as sending me poisonous shrubs and bugging my apartment for over four years. Would it be much of a stretch to assume that he's capable of far worse?

"I despise Heyworth Thorne," he admits. At the same time, he slips one of his hands around to my lower back as if to ensure I can't run from such a confession. "I loathe what he stands for—but the justice I seek can't be found if he's dead. Trust that I have no interest in hurting him physically."

"You just want to destroy his reputation," I surmise. "But why? I know about your brother, but there has to be more to it than that—"

"I will tell you," he swears. "But not like this, when you are panicked and hysterical." He brushes his hand along my forearm as if to use my trembling as evidence against me. "You need rest. I am going to take you back to my suite and tie you to the bed if I have to. You may even enjoy it, *¿sí?*"

"I can't…" An exhausted sigh nearly robs me of balance. I sway as he tightens his grip, steering me against his chest. For the first time, I notice the real world beyond him. Rain is lashing at the windows and a streak of lightning lances across his face, illuminating the tension in his jaw. "I can't sleep," I croak. "I can't think. I'm so damn tired."

"Fine. But staying here is obviously distressing to you." Through gritted teeth, he proposes, "So let me take you somewhere else—"

"No. What if—"

"Away from here," he continues to insist. "Look at me." He cups my cheek against his palm as thunder resonates through the walls. "You shouldn't be here alone. Not during a storm." Ironic, considering that his heat feels more destructive than anything lightning could inflict. "Let me take you somewhere else. Anywhere else."

"Why?" My voice lacks the taunt it should have. "It's not just the storms I'm afraid of. I'll never escape him. I'll never—"

"Enough." He lunges, but the act his lips inflict isn't a kiss. It's a kill shot. Swift and decisive, designed to shut me up. Distract.

Disorient.

And it works. Shock strips me of everything—thoughts, fears, common sense. All that remains is searing fire.

And I want to burn in it.

His touch is an inferno I eagerly throw myself into. Grunting, he captures my waist in both hands, igniting me through the thin silk of my robe. His tongue invades, his mouth conquers, and there's nothing I can do to withstand the onslaught but breathe.

So I do, inhaling all I can of Damien Villa. It's a dangerous game to play. With every frantic gasp of air, my chest meets his, causing my nipples to harden beneath the friction.

"Wait," he breathes, pulling back. "Just wait—"

"Please." I slide my hands down to his hips.

"*Mierda.*" His teeth nip the tip of my tongue in response, sending a jolt of alarm through my entire body. A warning.

Submit, Juliana. Let him regain control and this won't go any further.

My brain is more than willing to comply. My body, however, rebels.

"Please." I flex my fingers, sending each nail into the material of his shirt. In retaliation, he jerks me closer. Our mouths collide again, grappling for the upper hand.

No one wins. We wind up panting, openmouthed, in a standoff he decides to break by sweeping his thumb around to the tie of my robe.

"Interesting outfit choice, Ms. Thorne," he growls against my tongue as I curl my fingers into the waistband of his trousers. "Can't say I'm not impressed. But *easy*, sweet girl." He finds my fingers and gently moves them from his zipper. With a practiced twist of his fingers, he undoes the fastening himself. "Let me take care of you, *¿sí?* Close your eyes."

I obey, shutting out everything but him. The ragged sound of his breathing, the rasp of his heated skin over mine…

"That's it," he all but groans as my fingers brush his abdomen. "I'm not going anywhere."

God, the hoarse sound building in his throat resonates in my bones, so much more alarming than thunder. It's concession.

"I propose another bargain." He cups my chin, recapturing my mouth while his other hand fists itself into my hair, holding me captive for every searing, searching thrust of his tongue. Against my parted lips, he breathes, "You give me tonight. All those fears, your pain…it's all mine."

His deft fingers yank the material of my robe from my shoulders as he guides me back step by step. When my knees finally brush the edge of my mattress, he eases me down and my eyes flutter open just enough to take him in. A mixture of neon streetlights and lightning paints him in varying degrees of blues and yellows. He's abstract artwork too beautiful to ever own.

My fingers smooth down his torso anyway, sliding beneath his suit jacket to study him thoroughly. Rapid heartbeat. Formidable chest that vibrates as he snarls something into my open mouth.

He tenses the lower I go. Lower. Lower. *Jackpot.*

"Easy, *dulce niña.*" A warning exhale blows from his nostrils as my fingers find what I assume is a tailored pair of boxer briefs and… There's no mistaking what's beneath my palm. Heat. Fabric. Pulsing. Danger.

A knot in my belly tightens as I peel the cotton down bit by bit—but he was right. Watching him isn't enough. I make myself blind again, flicking my tongue along his jaw. God, it's like I can taste in his skin the things my eyes alone would never reveal. The spicy hint of excitement. The bitter tinge of irritation for not having complete control.

He is a toxin more potent than my dying oleander.

His fingers, dangerously soft, smooth over my hips, positioning me against him. The width of his knee starts to nudge my thighs apart and shock pierces through the fog in my brain.

"Easy, sweet girl." Before I can even tense, his mouth teases a moist trail from my jaw to my ear, nipping all the way. "Tell me to stop and I will," he murmurs against my earlobe.

His body advances where his mind shows restraint, however. Grasping hands drift between my legs, stroking a searing path along my inner thigh. When he slides his thumb along my core, air escapes my lungs in pitiful gasps. I writhe, drawing my knees together, easing them apart. I'm exposed to him like this, with no blindfold or distance to hide behind.

I have a first-row seat to how his nostrils twitch. My parted lips capture the hiss escaping his clenched teeth as his fingers find me slick and ready. The next kiss holds no mercy. No sanity. He gives. Takes. Bites.

"Mine," he growls, cupping my waist, urging me against him. "I knew you'd feel… *Mine.*"

With my eyes closed, I find his ear again, brushing my lips against the lobe. Words escape between pants. "Please —Please—"

He's gone. I blink, finding him on his knees, wrestling with the front of his trousers, tugging them off completely. My eyes go directly to the part of him I've only felt until now.

My lips part in awe. He's beautiful. He's terrible. A thickened ridge of flesh jutting to attention. Pulsing. For me. I reach out, curling my fingers around the swollen tip —but nothing could prepare me for how he feels: silk over steel.

"Lie back." With harsh, unsteady motions, he fishes a square silver package from his pocket. "Something told me to always be prepared when it comes to you," he says as if in answer to my questioning look. Upon bringing the wrapper to his teeth, he tears it open and slides the sheath along his length. Then he cups my ass in both hands and drags me to him.

My nails pierce the flesh of his shoulders and he sinks into me with the fervor of someone ripping open their collector toy, forsaking its value.

I cry out, flinching at the unexpected burning pressure as I'm spread open around him, forced to accept every inch. All of Damien Villa.

He's in my head, shutting out the world, and the storm, and memories, and everything but this. I'm in his skin, defacing him with hairline scratches and finger-shaped bruises.

His thumb finds the bundle of nerves above where we're joined and rubs. Fire. Sparks. Pleasure gradually replaces the discomfort and he silences my gasp with heated words of Spanish, his lips fluttering over mine, coaxing them apart.

I let him in and he lunges, matching each thrust of his hips with one of his tongue. Pinching pain quickly ebbs, giving way to a toe-curling sensation I can't name. Something too raw. Too sharp. Too burning. Too *much*.

My body grips him like a vise, my knees locking around his hips, guiding every move he makes. He only goes as deep as I let him. As fast as I need him to. It's a terrible, torturous courtesy, because I don't know what I want.

All I can do is move. And shudder. And whimper. And break.

Suddenly, he rips his mouth from mine and sinks his teeth along my jaw. "*Mierda*," he snarls, followed by a rush of grated nonsense. Promises. Threats. Dark things he wishes to do to me. Things he swears I'll *let* him do.

When he rears back for one last thrust, my hips arch to meet him, driving him so deep that I'm not sure where he ends and I begin.

Everything inside me tightens and releases like a rubber band snapping. My back bows. My eyes widen. Limp in the aftermath, I lie breathless as sanity returns in slow, fleeting snatches. I'm drenched in sweat. He has me pinned between cotton and flesh. The storm still rages around us, but his arms hold me tight, cocooning me from the rest of the world.

"Sweet...sweet girl." He's still panting. Startlingly hot fingers trace my cheek, demanding my attention. "Don't presume that this negates our agreement."

He grips me even tighter. Captured. The same way someone might lock his doll away for safekeeping until he decided to play with her again. A rumble of thunder partially obscures what he murmurs to me next. Something that should haunt whatever nightmares I dare to have.

"Exquisite. Too exquisite, sweet girl. In fact, I think I shall keep you after all…"

NINE

My Egyptian cotton duvet is worth fifteen hundred dollars and it doesn't compare to the comfort of being held. Heat, sweat, and Damien combined is a sensation that can't be packaged and sold. What a shame. A pleasant ache lingers in my muscles as I stretch my naked limbs, but I should feel guilt, I suppose. Disgust. Maybe those emotions would distract from the grim realization that has me opening my eyes to a dreary view of an overcast sky from beyond my windows.

I'm alone again.

A carefully folded note waits on my bedside table, but I don't bother reading it until I finally find the strength to stand.

The message is simple: *Had some business to attend to. Will return shortly.* At the bottom of the page, he painstakingly added, *PS: I have access to your medical records. I will have mine delivered.*

I swallow hard, uneasy at the implication. Not only has the bastard penetrated my life further, but he…

Well, he got what he wanted. Didn't he?

Thoughts of medical records aside, I drag myself into the shower and dress in the plainest clothing I can find: a black sweater and pants. After ripping my bedsheets from the mattress and tossing them into the hamper, I make my usual cup of coffee. Then I slam my fist into the counter so hard that I wind up crying out and clutching the damn thing to my chest.

What the hell have I done?

Why, I had sex with Damien Villa, of course. Sex with my father's archenemy while he's lying near death in a hospital bed. To put it even blunter: I gave him exactly what he wanted.

Perhaps he'll move on to the next bored, pathetic socialite? Instead of flowers today, I'll receive a calling card or two reminding me of his hate for my father outside my door.

Instead, I find a small ivory box on my welcome mat.

Inside it lies a delicate strip of pink silk covered in tiny, seemingly hand-painted roses. My fingers shake as I hold it upright. A beautiful custom blindfold sufficient enough to use in whatever game Damien may have in store for me next. I carry it and the box inside and place it somewhere within sight, remembering his promise to have my things brought to his place.

When a sharp, shrill tone cuts the silence, I barely recognize it as my cell phone. I answer it absently, but the voice on the other end snaps me from my daze.

"He's awake," Diane says through smothered sobs. "Juliana… He's finally awake."

I enter my father's hospital room unsure of what to expect. From my position near the doorway, I can tell he's still in bed. But one obvious change is impossible to miss. His eyes are open…

Only the expression in them doesn't belong to the charming, witty man I know. Dark-blue eyes sit like marbles in his skull, devoid of their usual sparkle. Instead, they're blank. Staring. Empty.

"Daddy?" I croak, inching closer.

"Juliana…" Diane rises from her vigil beside him and surreptitiously swipes at her bloodshot eyes with the sleeve of her sweater. "You came." The second I'm close enough, she throws her arms around me. "He doesn't respond much," she whispers near my ear. "He doesn't talk, but he may be able to hear you. The doctors aren't sure how long it may last… But it's progress." She smiles tearfully as if trying to convince herself of that fact. Progress.

"Daddy?" I circle around to his bed.

One of his frail, pale hands is resting over his chest, perched atop the blankets. I grab it, but he doesn't even look in my direction. Heyworth Thorne is gone, replaced by a shell.

Or the worst kind of villain: a helpless one. It's as if his goddamn soul is determined to withhold answers from me. Or punish me.

"I know this isn't the right moment," Diane says, lifting something from the bedside table: a stack of documents. "But just in case… You should be prepared. It's his will," she explains, holding the documents out to me. "Thank God we finalized it before—" She breaks off, clearing her throat. "I want you to look it over so that you aren't surprised if the worst comes to fruition."

"S-Surprised?" I scan the document, steeling myself for the worst scenarios my paranoia can dream up. Plenty. Perhaps he cut me out. He never intended to leave me a dime, not that the money matters in the grand scheme. If anything, a legal, binding document will prove that I was always his daughter merely for show. But as I scan the first lines, I shake my head. "This can't be right."

"It is," Diane insists, her eyes welling with tears. "We discussed it beforehand. It's what he wanted. But I think, all things considered, you should have access to some items now. I've already cleared it with the lawyer. They're highlighted there. A safety deposit box he had. I'm not sure what's in it, but you should have access to it."

I blink, fighting to resist how my eyes are burning. "I don't know what to say."

"There's something else." Diane grabs my arm.

For the first time, I sense how her fingers are shaking. Her distress takes on a new connotation; perhaps the tears aren't solely related to my father's condition.

"There might be tighter security when you come back. Family only. The police have opened an investigation. After the doctors ran more tests, they think the stroke may have been exacerbated by something."

"Exacerbated? Like…" I parse the clinical term and can only come up with one comparable to it. "He was poisoned?"

Her lips purse, her face pale. "I don't know. With all of the other reports… I'm terrified, Juliana. I know your father wanted extra security on you before he—"

"I'll be fine." I squeeze her hand reassuringly. "And I'll be back. I just…"

Need to breakdown, alone in a back stairwell, where no one can hear me sob openly into my palm. I thought Heyworth Thorne's death would be the hardest reality to face—but this is worse. So much worse. He's still here, his face the familiar one of my childhood hero. But in those blank, soulless eyes, all I saw was my reflection. My face. My guilt. This is all my fault.

He's gone because of me.

And a part of me still hates him for it.

TEN

With the city in turmoil over my father's recent scandal and subsequent health issues, there is only one place I can escape to find some semblance of peace.

I try not to feel guilty for invading it. As long as I inhale deeply, relishing the scent of hundreds of blooming flowers, it's surprisingly easy to. Peace seems attainable here—as long as I ignore the fact that I'm an intruder in this unique parallel universe. Its owner may make an exception for me though—for a price.

"I never allow anyone in here," he declares as he advances through the greenhouse, toward the section I'm standing in, sandwiched between nightshade and oleander. "And Julio usually abides by that rule. He must like you to risk upsetting me."

"Or he could just pity me. I'm crying," I say casually before he can deduce as much himself. "I'm upset. I'm...I'm a mess—"

"Because your father is awake."

It's pointless to ask how he knows that. Where my family is concerned, he seems to know everything.

"He is awake. If you can call it that." I finger the very edge of a petal of oleander, comparing the fresh bloom to the dying one in my apartment. The contrast is a stark parallel to my father's health: vitality vs. decay. "He couldn't even look at me. He can't speak. The doctors don't know if he'll ever fully recover. In fact, they're prepared for the worst." I rustle the documents clutched in my opposite fist. "Diane even gave me his will, just in case."

"I'm sorry," Damien says. His steps continue their slow, steady advance and I hate how my heart lurches at his presence. It's dangerous to grow attached to him. To need him. To crave the touch he runs along my lower back in quiet reassurance. "You may have full access to my legal team should you need their assistance."

"You don't understand. He left me everything." I can barely get the words out. "Everything. The house. His money. I don't understand. Did he love me or not? Was I his daughter or a trophy?"

Damien doesn't answer.

"The police think he may have been poisoned," I add. "Targeted by the same bad luck affecting every high-profile official who worked on your brother's case. They were even at my suite yesterday. Invading my privacy in the name of safety—"

"If this is an accusation…" He trails his thumb up to my neck, following the path of my throat. "It is a rather polite one, I must say. As far as cold-blooded murder is concerned, I've been accused of far worse with much less tact."

"Please." I squeeze my eyes shut, sensing every smooth, silken dip in the pad of his finger. "Don't lie to me," I beg. "You said you wanted honesty from me—but I need it from you."

"*Sí*," he agrees. "But first I must ask you directly: Do you really think that I would resort to murdering Heyworth Thorne, knowing how much he means to you still?"

It's a dangerous question and I loathe the way he asked it: in a strained, cautious tone. Like my answer matters to him more than anything else.

Even revenge.

"You hate him," I explain. "Maybe you have a good reason to. But if you care about me, even a fraction, you'd know… he's all I have." Fresh tears well in my eyes and spill down my cheeks, impossible to stop. "He's all I have. I can't lose him. I can't—"

"He had a reputation on the bench, especially back then," Damien says gruffly. "For being fair. Just. A judge who would hear all facts and rule with honesty."

I force myself to nod. *That* is the Heyworth Thorne I grew up with—a man admired in his interpretation of the law.

"But as I sat in that courtroom, with Mathias' life at stake, I saw a different man," Damien confesses, his tone level. The deliberate lack of anger somehow makes his words cut deeper. "A reckless tyrant too interested in bold headlines to actually listen. To fucking see. *Sí*, I saw a fraud too prideful to make the judgment the facts demanded."

"The jury convicted him," I point out. "My father would have upheld it. He wouldn't overrule a guilty verdict."

"I have the case files," he says. "I'll let you read them."

And in some ways, it's a more terrifying prospect than having him try to convince me on his own. More words. More exposed lies. Can I handle them?

"But not tonight. I've humored you enough. You need to eat. I'm taking you to dinner."

"Oh?" I incline my head to view him from over my shoulder. "Is that a command?"

"No." His lips twitch, fighting a smile. "Think of it as more of a request. A stern request in the interest of your welfare. And some selfishness as well. We need to discuss what happened last night."

"Hmm?" I feign ignorance. "About the storm?"

He smiles for real, but there's no warmth in it. An intensity wafts from him instead, more unnerving than his polished, suave charm. "I'd prefer to discuss the sex, if you don't mind."

I cough, clearing my throat. "I—"

"I would like to extend our arrangement as well," he says over me. "In case you thought I desired only your virginity."

"You don't?" I ask hoarsely. "I mean…you didn't?"

"*Sí.*" He frowns, stroking his chin with the tip of his thumb. "It seems I desire more when it comes to you than initially anticipated."

"Like what?"

"Well…" He circles my position, allowing one of his hands to molest a budding flower as he goes. "I'd very much like to feel my cock inside of you again, for one."

"Oh?" I squeak as fire sears my cheeks. "How bold of you to say, Mr. Villa."

"*Sí.*" He takes another step in my direction. "Bold. As is the fact that I know you enjoyed feeling said cock inside of you. In fact…" He's close enough now to cup my cheek with his palm, tilting my face into his touch. "I believe I've discovered a more enticing conquest than your innocence."

A second's pause is my cue to reply.

"W-What?"

"Your fear of the dark." His nostrils flare as if chasing that elusive prize. "Oh, *sí*, I want to take it," he tells me. "Own it. Shape it. You will never hear another thunderstorm without thinking of me."

I close my eyes as the full extent of his promise resonates. No more fear. No night terrors. No Simon.

"And if I refuse?" I wonder, daring to open my eyes again. He's still here, alarmingly intent. This isn't a dream. Painfully real, his heat assaults my skin, awakening parts of me I've felt stir only at his touch. His whim.

"I don't think you will," he says, confident. "In fact, I think you might enjoy this conquest more than the first."

I draw in a ragged breath at the memory. The slickness of his skin. The friction between us. The way the world faded, reduced to him alone.

"I should have you sussed by now. In fact, sex should have concluded my interest in you," he adds, the grit in his tone drawing me from my thoughts. "And yet, at every damn turn, you…confound me."

Confound? I bite my lip against a retort. I'm sure he has no trouble sensing my emotions regardless. My chest is heaving against the barely-there barrier of my clothing, my breaths fanning the air.

"I'm reckless with you," he adds as warm breath nudges my throat, alluding to just how close he is now. "You make me…impulsive when I should have a steadying hand. And you know damn well what I mean."

He stills right when another gained inch would press him against me—yet he's near enough for me to inhale his scent and exhale resolve.

"Do I?"

"*Sí.*" Rare tension sows ripples through his polished baritone. "I expected you quivering and fearful beneath me. Maybe then I could draw the real woman lurking behind the polished façade. I'd make her talk to me."

His hands smooth up my spine from behind, locking me into place. With only a thin bit of fabric as a shield, my body is his plaything. Trembling. Alight. Ignoring my commands to run.

"I'm tired of being afraid, Mr. Villa," I say.

"As if you ever were. Last night, I realized the truth."

I stiffen as his lips ghost the side of my throat, beneath my ratty hair.

"I've been sending you the wrong flower, Ms. Thorne. You're no rose—you're a vine. You grow there in the midst of the weeds, your stem slightly crooked, your petals lacking the uniform nature of all the other flowers. At a glance, you look like the rest. But if someone were to feel…"

He performs that very action as the words leave his throat, sliding his hands up my back, cinching the thin material of my dress beneath his fingers. "They'd realize the truth. Your thorns are sharper. Your petals are softer. Your smell is different." His fingers shake. Grasping. Pulling.

Focusing on his words is hard enough, let alone keeping my balance. I sway.

"I could spend years painting you and never learn more than I did last night just by being inside of you."

Does that infuriate him? Yes. I can hear the scowl in his voice. Damien Villa, the artist so used to deciphering his subjects and throwing them away. I confound him.

But he mystifies me.

"I may even rethink my boundary when it comes to the club," he adds, his voice lowering, just for me to hear. "I could fuck you in front of them all. Let them see: I'm the only man who will know how it feels to have you come on his cock. Like heaven." His palm flexes against my cheek as the thumb of his opposite hand grazes my lower lip. "Exquisite."

I'm too breathless to question. Speak. Inhale. All I can do is savor the sensation of his heat on my skin. His breath mingling with mine. The growl he bites down as I step into him, letting him feel every inch I can press into his flesh.

"Beautiful girl," he praises, his lips grazing my ear before drifting lower. "Beautiful, sweet...*mine*." With a predatory intent, he finds the exposed flesh, raking with his teeth. Grasping with his nails.

A moan slips from my lips, my head falling back.

It's like he's aware of every sordid thought before I even think it. His mouth finds mine easily. As if he memorized the distance. He exhales at the taste of me, slipping his tongue between my lips. Drinking me in. One word grated against my mouth reveals his impression.

"Maddening. The way you sound... It's sinful. I can tell from one note if you are in pain. Pleasure. Ecstasy. No one else has such range."

As if to prove it, his hand finds my breast, stroking the aching peak through chafing cotton.

"I knew from the moment I heard your voice—really heard it—that I was going to count the many ways I could make you scream."

Another kiss drowns me in him. His scent. His touch. He steers me back until I'm trapped between him and a wall of glass, his to devour. Consume.

"And your smell," he breathes as his hand travels lower, dancing down my belly, hunting for the hem of my dress. "It's so damn easy to tell when you're aroused."

He succeeds in lifting my skirt, finding my thigh without preamble. Featherlight caresses track his progress upward, nearing the space between my legs. I stiffen. He pounces, plunging a finger beneath the gusset of my panties.

"*Sí*," he croaks, inhaling the air while curling his finger in the same cruel motion. "It's like you were designed for me. To entice me. To challenge me. To humble me… You've punished me, haven't you?" He practically hisses the words. "Every sin. Every transgression. You've made me repent."

His thumb roughly encircles me—my only warning before he plunges the tip between my folds. My sharp cry almost drowns out his next words.

"*Dulce niña.*" He slides his hand around to my back and the faint hum of a zipper sounds as the fabric of my dress loosens. Falls. Exposes.

Trembling knees threaten to collapse beneath me. I grab his shoulders tighter, marveling at the ease with which he supports me. One hand braced against my ass allows him to steady me while guiding my hips against his at the same time.

A gasp rips from my throat at the dangerous pressure kicking against my belly. He returns his attention to exploring my body, his touch bolder. He spreads my legs apart, tracing soft, nonsensical patterns into my inner thigh. The gentleness with which he does so sends my already drifting thoughts scattering further. There's reverence in his touch and I have an uncomfortable inkling why so many women have been willing to strip naked for him in the first place.

Someone else could never offer this level of intimacy. A vulnerability found only by having a stranger peer beneath your skin with every stroke.

I close my eyes, savoring the small nuances he can't disguise. The low grunts interspersed with his breaths. The pulsing heat. The thick fingers tangling in my hair, making knots and chaos in the strands. Eyesight would only be a hindrance to him—because without it, he has no trouble sensing the secrets within I've hidden from myself. Sex extends to more than physical pleasure where he is concerned.

It's knowledge.

It's power.

It's primal.

"You wanted to be kept, and I've decided…that I'm keeping you." He slips an arm around my waist, wrenching me even closer.

My legs part as he muscles in between them. My knees capture his waist, holding tight—and I've surrendered to his strength completely.

"Maybe I would have played your game before," he admits before grinding his lips into mine, marking them. "Perhaps. I'd let you go. Let you taunt me like you have. I could withstand it."

"And now?" I'm copying him, grazing my lips along his jaw in return, sensing the barest hint of stubble.

"Too late." He sounds almost as if he pities me. "I want too much, so I'll take all of you."

"By spying on me again?" How I've formed a coherent reply, I'll never know.

"I won't have to."

Oh? A morbidly amusing thought comes to mind, even as my thoughts dissipate as he slides his fingers along my core and mutters something that makes my cheeks flame. Something about *wet*, mingled with broken words in Spanish. "Will you tie a bell around me?"

He laughs. "Maddening woman with maddening ideas."

He finds my panties again and tugs them aside. Every slow, deliberate stroke he inflicts reminds me of a musician playing an instrument only he bothered to learn how to tune.

And I'm pathetic enough to beg for more. "Damien." My lips seek out his earlobe. "Please…"

His breath stutters. The hum of a zipper pierces the air and then he's inside me. Sharp, sweet pleasure instantly displaces any pain. God, he feels so raw from this angle. There's nothing between us but sweat and skin. I can feel his heartbeat hammering a melody mine has no choice but to match.

Thump.

Stutter.

Thump.

He goes more slowly than any man has the right to, sensing every curve and ridge of my body, learning me inside and out. Too thoroughly. It's a violation I never in a million years thought I'd crave.

Teeth gritted, thighs clenched, I let him explore, thrust after deliberate thrust.

Far too soon, he loses his polish, gripping me hard enough to leave marks. Bruises. Brands.

Hissed words of Spanish meet their doom in the crook of my shoulder as his body tenses, slamming into mine and knocking the air from my lungs. God, the friction…

I'm ashes beneath the onslaught. Fire. Heat. Sin.

My world is a collage of sensation of blinding white.

Then silence and a slow descent back to reality.

"Damn," he grates between panting breaths as my senses reassemble. "That's not quite how I imagined the second time we met like this would unfold, Ms. Thorne."

My heart flutters, walking that dangerous line between dread and excitement. "What…what do you mean?"

He laughs, and any doubts are shattered. "I'd thought for sure we'd at least make it to the goddamn bed."

"*I* should be taken out and shot," Damien growls as his fingers dance along the flat of my belly. As if supplying accompanying percussion, a series of garbled, protesting noises rumble from it. "You're starving." He sighs against the back of my throat. "Perhaps I should have insisted on dinner first after all?"

I echo his sigh and lean further into him, relishing the feel of his chest against the curves of my back. Given the warm temperature of the greenhouse, his heat should be an unwelcome addition—but I shift closer, aching to extend the burn of his flesh on mine. Even the floor, slightly damp from the humidity, feels more comfortable than it has any right to.

"I don't want to move," I admit, cringing from the idea of putting my dress on and reentering the real world. Or pretending that what just happened didn't. "I want to lie here naked and never get up again."

"Never?" he wonders in a throaty chuckle. "May I propose a compromise?"

More like an ultimatum, it seems as he pulls away. I turn to watch him sit upright in a graceful arrangement of limbs. Seemingly from nowhere, he withdraws a headset from the tangled mass of clothing beside us.

"Julio," he says into the device. Spanish deepens the distance between us as he dishes out what I assume are a multitude of commands. Then he sets the headset aside and reaches toward our clothing again. "You do not have to move," he says, "But I would like you covered *por favor*."

He feels through the fabric and retrieves not my crumpled dress but his tailored suit jacket. Sitting up, I shudder as he drapes me in the fabric, easily maneuvering my arms into the sleeves.

He doesn't extend the same modesty to himself, however, not even as Julio calls from the door minutes later.

"Sir?"

"Yes," Damien replies. "The atrium, if you please."

Heavy footsteps advance across the far end of the greenhouse, but I never see the faithful bodyguard enter this section at least. A few moments later, the steps retreat.

"All done, sir."

"Thank you, Julio." Once he's sure his servant is gone, Damien stands and extends his hand toward me. "Slight movement, I'm afraid," he admits. "But I promise it will be well worth the effort."

I grasp his hand and allow him to pull me to my feet. Showing no concern for our discarded clothing, he starts forward, fearlessly navigating the aisles of flowers. I notice his hand feeling along the various stands, orienting himself, I suspect. But there's an unmistakable familiarity that makes me envision him spending so much time in here that he's memorized every inch.

"How is this for compromise?" he wonders as we reach the threshold of a large, open space beyond the main greenhouse. The same area he brought me the first time we had dinner here. Then, it served as a makeshift pizza parlor —and a chilling backdrop to a lurid conversation revolving around my virginity and his insane brother Mateo.

Now, the place reads Damien Villa down to the black tablecloth draped over a wooden table, laden with steaming plates.

"Five-star French restaurant to go?" I inquire, eyeing the pastries and extravagant cuisine.

He laughs and advances toward the table, angling one of the chairs toward me.

Once we're seated, we eat in relative silence, him unabashedly naked still. Observing him now reveals more than ever before. He lazily munches on the end of a croissant, but his true focus is tracing the veins on the back of the hand I have braced on the table.

"You are so beautiful," he murmurs heatedly. "*Hermosa niña—*"

"How can you tell?" I blurt, only to realize how rude it sounds. "I mean… Are you merely aiming to flatter me, Mr. Villa?"

"No." His tone dips an octave, suddenly serious. He captures my hand entirely, lifting it for his physical inspection. His thumb grazes the flat of my palm as if the divots and swirls there can tell him all he needs to know. "Your body is a masterpiece. One I hope to explore in full."

"You do still owe me a painting," I point out.

He laughs. "Yes." He lifts his head in my direction. "And answers. You can demand them from me now, if you want."

"No," I say, surprising myself. "Not now. Tomorrow. Just let me have a few more hours of pretending if it's not too much trouble."

"Trouble?" He brings my hand to his lips, pressing them along my knuckles. "Never."

"Let's just hope we aren't interrupted this time," I say. The way his jaw twitches is the only clue I need to know I've said the wrong thing. "I'm sorry—"

"Don't be." A heart-stopping grimace twists his lips, part frown, part…smile? "Mateo is, let's just say slow to warm to new people. He was always that way. But there is no malice in his hostility." He shrugs, his jaw softening a fraction. "In some aspects, he is like a child. Painfully demanding, but affectionate to those who earn it. Though it seems he is more of the former around me lately."

"He made you trade him something to stay away from me," I surmise, licking my lips. "Didn't he?"

His head shoots up, cocked to the side. "It seems I didn't give him enough."

"Did you?" I press.

"Perhaps." A muscle in his neck flutters, and he shakes his head. "Fine. I gave him control over a facet of our mutual business arrangements. Let's leave it at that."

I look down, eyeing the table as an uncomfortable sensation floods my belly. Gratitude? "You didn't have to—"

"You don't know Mateo," he says over me. "It appears we both have complicated relationships with our family members, ¿sí?"

"That sounds…relatable," I admit, fighting to sound cordial.

"Pardon the cliché, but I would blame our upbringing," Damien admits. "Our father was not an easy man to live with. Mateo learned that more than most."

"Oh?"

"What is a polite way to say… He favored corporal punishment."

"I'm sorry."

"Again, you do not have to be. It wasn't a terrible life in a sense. I'm grateful for it."

"H-How did you leave?"

A thoughtful grunt catches in his throat. "Our mother was American. So my brothers and I had dual citizenship through her—making us technically citizens, not immigrants. The media tends to skew some facts." His cold, quick smile takes my breath away. A heartbeat later, it's gone, smothered into a flattened line.

"You grew up in Colombia though," I point out, recalling what my father mentioned. "Supposedly, Mr. Villa, you are linked to the drug trade."

"*Sí*, supposedly," he admits. "My father owned a ranch of sorts. We tended the fields. He grew an array of unusual crops. Only later did I realize that the plants we grew supplied a criminal enterprise. Allegedly, of course."

Like his supposed links to cocaine.

"I'm sure you did what you had to do to survive," I say carefully. "I know what that's like."

"Oh?" He chuckles. "Maybe I've lost that ruthless drive. After all, I've just alluded to illegal activity in front of the daughter of an ex-judge."

He expertly mingles fact with the veiled threat. Though a part of me suspects it's more of a test. He's deliberately spoon-feeding me key bits of information that, if leaked to the press, don't confirm or deny the rumors. Smart man. Perhaps too smart.

"I think you're calculating, Mr. Villa," I tell him truthfully, still tracing an invisible path over the back of his hand. "You wouldn't let anything compromising slip around a potential threat, no matter how much you may enjoy getting her naked."

"Ah, but that's where you're wrong, Ms. Thorne. It seems I repeatedly find myself saying things around you that I shouldn't."

"Like?"

"For instance, would you believe that I have never mentioned my past to anyone?" His tone lowers in an accusatory fashion. Like I'm to blame for his slip of the tongue. "Even in such admittedly sparse detail."

"You mean you've never told your past women"—I deliberately pick three names at random—"Christina, Babina, and Martina, about your childhood?"

"No." He slides his hand from beneath mine only to capture my fingers entirely. As I watch, he runs his thumb along my palm. "I haven't. They never held my interest beyond what I sought to learn from them."

Learn. A nice way of phrasing sex. "And what about me? Do I hold your interest?"

He frowns as if hating his answer before it even leaves his mouth. "I'm afraid to admit that you have my full attention."

"For now," I say coyly. "But who knows how long that may last? Maybe as long as one of your pretty roses?"

"I'm afraid not." His grip tightens. "If only it were that simple, Ms. Thorne." He stands.

I balk. His free hand brushes the table for guidance as he circles it toward me, and a tug on my wrist urges me to my feet. One ruthless yank pulls me close and his lips flutter over mine. Once. Twice. On the third brush, mine fall open by accident, letting him in. Urging him deeper. My fingers are in his hair before I can help myself. God, it's softer than his skin. Like silk. Vaguely, I'm aware of the edge of the table striking my hip as he steers me to face him. Before I realize it, I'm sliding back onto the ledge.

"Wait." I break the kiss, panting for air. "S-Stop."

He does, his breath feathering my throat in heavy, unsteady bursts as I curl my fingers around his biceps, intending to shove him off. Clear my head. Think. He muscles in closer instead. Silverware scatters, sliding dangerously close to the table's edge.

"I'm merely following your rules, Ms. Thorne," he says into my throat. "You desire to be kept—as well as distracted. I aim to oblige."

I wake up twisted within the silk sheets of that infamous red room. As my eyes open, the mirror on the ceiling paints my appearance in stark relief: swollen, bitten lips, a nest of hair, and a hollow, sallow face.

My phone is ringing. It has been almost nonstop for the past five minutes, but I can't seem to move to grab it. At least not until the millionth ring when I finally crawl off the mattress.

"Juliana," Diane says when I answer, her voice strained. "We… Can you come to the hospital? We need to talk."

"What's happened?" Fear rides a wave of nausea threatening to escape from my throat. "Is he—"

"No, no, your father is fine," she says quickly. "It's just… There are some arrangements we need to go over. Just come down when you can."

After hanging up, I shower and then dress in the plainest items of clothing to be found in Damien's mocking wardrobe: a white shirt and beige slacks. As I enter the foyer, I don't find him lounging on the leather chaise or lurking in the corners.

But on a table near the door, someone left a gray folder with a single rose draped across it. Printed in ominous black font are the words *Borgetta Murder Case*. Swallowing hard, I tuck the file beneath my arm and slip the rose behind my ear.

Ten minutes later, I'm racing down the hall outside my father's hospital room, my stomach in knots. Inside, Diane is sitting beside Daddy's bed, his hand in hers. He lies motionless, his eyes open and unseeing—but standing nearby is a tall, mustached man I don't recognize.

At least not until Diane says, "This is Chief Harrison, Juliana. A good friend of your father's." Her strained, uneasy smile makes me force one in return.

"Hello, chief." I step forward, vaguely pairing the man's stern features with a face I've only seen in the papers or on the periphery of Daddy's lavish political gatherings throughout the years.

He has a relatively prominent family from what I recall. His son is a promising lawyer, his wife a defense attorney. Dressed formally, he certainly matches his job title. A brown trench coat hangs open to reveal the badge pinned to his crisp white dress shirt, and the faint hint of cigar smoke tinges his imposing frame. My nostrils wrinkle and I can't shake a chilling sense of déjà vu. Maybe I'm forgetting a more recent meeting?

"Juliana." He extends his hand for mine and shakes it before I can ponder my memories further. "I'm so sorry to hear about what happened. My men and I are doing all we can to help."

"The police would like your permission to secure your apartment, darling," Diane says, cutting to the chase. "They've already been at the house. For our safety."

"S-Safety?" I raise an eyebrow.

"Yes." Chief Harrison steps back, his eyes downcast. "I'm sorry to be the one to tell you this, Juliana, but your father's physicians believe that his stroke may have been caused by something he could have ingested—they aren't sure what yet. But I want to assure you that we are doing our best to get to the bottom of it."

"The tests haven't come back yet," Diane explains as we turn to daddy in unison. "But your father would want you safe."

"That's why your officers were at my suite the other day?" I ask, fighting to keep the suspicion from my tone. "For my safety?"

"I apologize if their presence alarmed you," the chief says. "But given your recent association with Damien Villa, I know your father would want your security to be of the utmost priority."

I swallow hard and struggle to keep my tone cordial. "My association?" Judging from the barely concealed hostility in his tone, this man shares the same view of Damien that my father did. *Does.* "Is he a suspect?"

"I didn't mean to insult you," Chief Harrison says, but his expression doesn't reveal an ounce of contrition. His eyes rake over me, lingering near my throat and the pearl hanging there. "I know your father tended to shelter you. You can't be blamed for not understanding just how dangerous such a man may be. Even I am forced to mingle with him on occasion."

"Because of rumors?" I innocently question.

He smiles. "Tell me. Have you ever heard of *La Muerte*?"

I shake my head. "No, I haven't."

"As you wouldn't. You're a smart woman, but I doubt you've spent much time researching Colombian gangs. It means the order of the death," he says. "One of the more dangerous outfits to operate below the border. In fact, one of its former leaders was rumored to have run something of a cult—killed a few years ago."

"Interesting," I manage to croak.

"Very," Harrison agrees. "Even more interesting is the fact that some of the rumors state that the Villa boys are none other than that man's sons, continuing their legacy so to speak. And if that rumor has any merit to it at all, you have no idea what such a family may be capable of."

But maybe he's wrong. Damien himself alluded to that very possibility: *Maybe I've lost that ruthless drive.*

"This is all a precaution, Juliana," Diane insists. "Just in case."

"I should be going anyway." Chief Harrison nods toward Diane and extends his hand in my direction. "I'll keep in touch, Juliana. I hope to see you at the gala as well." His grip tightens harder than I expect as he swiftly shakes my hand and then releases it. "Best of luck."

I watch him go, rubbing the hand he touched against my pants. It's throbbing.

"Gala?" I ask, looking back at Diane.

"That's what I wanted to talk to you about," she admits, wringing her slim fingers together. "Chief Harrison offered to stand in, but I think you should. You should represent your father at the annual Wellington benefit gala."

The Wellington family has a long history in the city's political landscape. I think one of them was a presidential candidate, and several have served as senators or prominent businessmen. The last one to make a mark is the youngest son of their last influential patriarch: a man more inclined to dole out money to politicians than mingle among them. He died a few years back of a heart attack, but Daddy still attended every year, kissing up to the executors of his estate.

"I've never been," I say thickly. "He never took me."

"It's tomorrow night," Diane says. "Your father was a headliner. He planned to secure donations—" She breaks off, swallowing hard. "Please. *You* should represent him. It's what he—no, it's what I want. Please, Juliana."

I've never seen her like this, her eyes bloodshot, her hands trembling.

"All right." I step forward and carefully throw my arms around her, hugging her tight. "I'll go. Don't worry."

She squeezes me in return. "Thank you. Thank you. I know he'd… Thank you. And"—she pulls back and swipes a wayward lock of hair away from my face—"I hope whatever your father left for you gave you some ounce of closure."

I lower my gaze to my purse, remembering the documents tucked inside it. "I haven't gone yet," I admit. "But I will."

*J*ulio is waiting for me at the hospital's private entrance, standing beside the car. Without complaint, I enter the back seat, but as the faithful bodyguard takes the wheel, I clear my throat.

"Damien put you in charge of my security," I start, settling my hands primly on my lap.

"*Sí.*" The man shoots me a wary glance from the corner of his eye. "Can I help you with anything, Ms. Thorne?"

"I want to take a detour," I propose. "A detour without getting approval from your boss first. A *personal* detour that I'm informing you about rather than running off on my own."

"So, if I may ask, why are you?" Amusement laces Julio's otherwise professional tone.

A smile tugs on my mouth as well—at least until I mull over his question. "Because I'm scared," I admit, turning to stare out the window as the city streets pass in a blur. "I'm terrified, enough that I would rather not shun one of the few people capable of protecting me."

"So where to, Ms. Thorne?"

I bite back a sigh of relief. Will he really keep this quiet? I have no choice but to take the risk. "A bank," I say, fishing a stack of documents from my purse. "Here is the address."

He nods, and moments later, we arrive in front of an upscale establishment in the heart of the city. When I approach a woman at the front desk, she eyes me warily until I say what must be the magic words.

"I'm Juliana Thorne. My father has a security deposit box here?"

"Oh, yes! Your mother called the other day." She rummages through a desk drawer and withdraws a small silver key, which she places within my reach. "They're in the alcove just past the security guard. The number is on the key."

I follow her instructions, my heart racing as I wonder what could be inside the harmless structure. Each security deposit box is small, built into the wall, and no larger than a shoebox. Nearby, other people hunch over their private sections, rummaging through their belongings before locking them away.

When I finally gather the nerve to open my father's box, I don't find a glaring item labeled *Evidence of Simon*. In fact, the only items here to discover are a genuine diamond necklace belonging to his first wife, Bethany, who died when I was nine, and legal documents that look like they pertain to the ownership of the house and other properties. Frowning, I strain on tiptoe and slide my hand over the inside of the box. Just when I start to withdraw it, my fingers strike something soft and crinkly—a single piece of paper.

It's a handwritten note, but one penned hastily on official letterhead. It's old and weathered, but I can make out the barely legible font of the city's precinct underneath a logo. *J. Mirangas*, someone wrote. *Age 8. Morrison, PA. 10/28.*

A wave of nausea washes over me and I have to brace my hand against the wall and close my eyes to steel myself against the onslaught. The page is a crumpled mass in my fist, but I can't loosen my grip. I can't even breathe.

My name. Someone from this police department—in another state, let alone jurisdiction from my old hometown —gave Heyworth information on my case. Supposedly, he was asked to consult by the Morrison police chief. So why would another official from a city hours away have written my name down on a paper destined to collect dust in Heyworth Thorne's private bank?

"Miss?" The security guard outside of the alcove stands in the doorway, watching me. "Are you okay?"

"I'm fine." Forcing a smile, I return everything to the deposit box and lock it. "Can I keep the key?" I ask the girl at the front desk, who nods.

"Sure! Access to the alcove is available twenty-four-seven," she chirps. "Just present your ID to the guard."

"Any more detours, Ms. Thorne?" Julio inquires as I meet him beside the car.

"Not at the moment," I say while climbing into the back seat. I wait for him to reclaim the wheel before I add, "But can I trust you to keep this little trip between us?"

Even more so now. Not because I don't trust Damien with what little information I learned, but I don't think I can say it out loud and parse its meaning. Not now. I don't even have the energy to flip through the file he left for me, either; it's still lying untouched on the seat.

"We might have an agreement," Julio says, surprising me. "But in return, I will need a favor from you."

"Oh?" I bite my lip, curious about what someone seemingly so loyal could want in return for deceiving his boss.

"You may have noticed that it is…easy to forget Mr. Villa's physical limitations," he says. "*¿Sí?*"

I nod. "He does seem fairly capable."

"And in some ways, it is easy to forget that he is not invincible. Human. I think even he has forgotten that at times."

I picture the suave, confident artist and find myself agreeing.

"Being around you is good for him," Julio admits. "He's had several women he's strung along—but you are the only one who talks to him like he is a man. The only one who punishes him when he upsets you and makes him seek your forgiveness. You challenge him, and I think he needs that more than anything. Friction. Resistance. Challenge. It makes him remember how to interact."

"Because he's used to getting his way," I surmise, recalling Chief Harrison's not-so-subtle insinuation.

"You see a different side of him," he admits. "A side I'd almost forgotten existed. The other Mr. Villa…" He makes a low sound in his throat and shakes his head. "Trust me, he is a man you have not seen, and you do not want to."

But maybe I have. A man who sent me oleander as a warning and broke into my apartment when he assumed I'd insulted him by merely buying his painting.

"He can be dangerous," I say thickly. "Can't he?"

"Can't we all?" He shrugs. "I like to think of him as not cruel, but transactional. So many people demand so much of him…he's come to see the world as a game, where he must be on his guard at all times."

"Demand," I echo. "Like who? His brother?" It's a stab in the dark. One that seems to hit a bull's-eye.

"Mateo," he hisses. "You'd do best to never interact with him."

So he isn't aware of Mateo's impromptu meeting after all.

"Mateo is dangerous," he adds. "In this world, he only sees himself. No one else."

"Why are you telling me this?" I feel my eyebrows furrow. "As secretive as Damien is, I doubt he'd approve of his loyal bodyguard spilling even a hint of his personal life."

Which means that this is about more than a petty bribe for his silence.

"Because I want you to understand," Julio says, proving as much. "If he hurts you—Mr. Villa—and he may—don't forgive him easily, if you decide to at all. Make him earn it. Make him feel it. I fear that may be the only way for him to learn, *sí*."

"Learn what?"

He cocks his head to look back at me, forsaking the road. "The risk," he says before turning away. "The risk that comes with losing something you value due to your own actions—when no amount of money in the world can salvage the damage. The only way to fix it is to open your heart."

"And you think he might hurt me?" I question.

"*Sí*. He will—*mierda*!" He slams his fists onto the horn as a car cuts in front of us. Growling through his teeth, he adds, "But he will not mean to, that I am sure of. I doubt he will even realize it."

It's an ominous warning. One that resonates as I watch the cityscape pass in a collage of flashing streetlights and oblivious people.

A warning that, oddly enough, doesn't make me feel threatened. More like…

Resigned. Because deep down, maybe a part of me has known all along that whatever exists between me and Damien was doomed from the start. Even his brother felt obligated to warn me.

And perhaps there is a twisted peace in that.

TWELVE

*J*ulio escorts me to the penthouse suite and ushers me inside. There, Damien is sitting in the living room, on a leather chaise positioned near the windows. If I didn't know better, I'd assume his pensive posture was due to appreciation of the amazing view of the city bathed in amber sunlight.

"How do you feel?" he wonders without moving from his relaxed position: legs outstretched, arms sprawled out beside him. It's such a contrast to his usual poised rigidity that I'd smile if his expression weren't so stern.

"I'm fine," I lie, placing his untouched file back where I found it this morning. Shadow drapes the cover, adding an ominous aura to the truths it may contain.

"Your father's condition is stable," he says, deploying his uncanny knowledge of my every move.

Intentionally? A hard swallow can't displace my unease. Does Julio really intend to keep our little secret? Something I sensed in his tone holds the paranoia at bay—concern. Damien may be his employer, but he cares about him.

"The doctors seem convinced he may recover with little complications," Damien adds.

"For now," I agree, crossing the room to join him. The moment I sit, his hand finds mine, placing it on the ridge of his knee. "But there is an open investigation. They think… he may have been poisoned."

It feels so strange to say it out loud. So surreal. For all of my father's obsessive paranoia, I never truly believed something like this could happen. That someone could want him dead.

How ironic that a prime suspect might be seated beside me.

Damien's grip tightens as if he's sensing my thoughts. "You can accuse me, if it helps," he suggests, admitting as much. "But trust me when I say I did not harm your father. Not in this instance."

I raise an eyebrow. "This instance?"

A muscle in his jaw lurches as he turns my hand so the palm is upright. "I may have attempted to persuade his donors away from supporting him," he confesses. "I may have mounted an ad campaign to thwart his chances at reelection. And I *may* be funding his opposition…"

"But?" I prompt, sensing one.

A sudden tightness hardens his expression. "But I would never kill him."

And I want to believe that, more than I have the right to.

"You did not read the file," he adds, catching me off guard.

"I…"

"I'm not insulted," he says. "It's funny. Something told me you wouldn't."

"Because I need to hear it from you." I shift, gently detangling my hand from his. In the same motion, I run my fingers along his jaw, amazed at just how welcoming he can feel. Beneath the cold, sometimes ominous demeanor, he's silk under my fingertips, a wealth of contradictions. "So tell me. What happened to Mathias?"

"We should start with Emily Borgetta," he suggests, tilting his chin into my touch. "A beautiful, if flirtatious, young girl with a wealth of besotted suitors at her disposal. Heirs to various fortunes, diplomats, the son of a police chief, even. As the daughter of a prominent businessman, the world was at her disposal. At least until the day she was found murdered in her apartment, possibly raped. Nothing was stolen, therefore making the crime far more heinous: personal in nature."

"Your brother was the only suspect," I say, scouring what few shreds of information I know about the case. "They were dating."

"He wasn't the only suspect." As if settling in for a long story, Damien rearranges himself, leaning back into the cushions of the chaise. His hand finds mine again, gripping tighter in a subtle way that warns I won't break free easily. "She had other suitors. Other men in her life who were questioned. But *Mathias* was the only one arrested, the poor *malparido* immigrant—at least that's what the reporters crowed. Even if he was a citizen as much as the rest. Even if there was no DNA linking him to the crime. No real conclusive *evidence*. Out of the rich, white suspects, he had the brownest skin."

"But there was enough there that a jury found him guilty," I point out.

"Guilty," he agrees. "But tell me why the expert witness who could testify as to the validity of the lack of DNA was barred from testifying? Why evidence of Emily Borgetta's phone records and a list of her prior lovers weren't allowed into evidence? Why the fact that Mathias had been questioned for nearly forty-eight hours straight in a nonstop barrage by the police department was not allowed to be presented in front of the jury?" He pauses, letting every bitter accusation sink in.

"Why not?" I ask, hating a part of me that already knows the answer.

"Every decision in that aspect was up to one person who consistently ruled against the interest of Mathias: Heyworth Thorne. His reasons are difficult to parse, but I believe that it was for personal gain. Someone powerful had an interest in closing the murder case quickly. Mathias was an easy scapegoat and Heyworth Thorne the willing pawn."

"I want to deny that, but..." I swallow hard, eyeing the city beyond this room. "But I think I'm starting to wonder if my adoption was more than a merciful whim on his part. What if he picked me because..." God I can't even say it. My fingers tremble in his grip, and I rake my free hand through my hair, twisting the strands. "What if he's the reason Simon was always able to find me on my birthday? What if he gave him access to me? What if all this time—"

"You're upsetting yourself," Damien warns. His thumb traces my cheek, capturing the tears he shouldn't be able to sense.

I'm not sobbing openly for once. I'm just…numb.

"Diane wants me to fill in for him at a benefit gala," I croak. "She wants me to smile, and pretend, and reassure his donors in his absence. She wants me to lie for him, but I'm not sure if I can."

"The Wellington gala?" he wonders, unsurprisingly correct. "Ironic in a way. Gerald Wellington was nothing more than an odd recluse who had an obsession with 'purity.' He seemed to think that there was no such thing as innocence. That even the most sheltered and pure harbored dark intentions. One merely need magnify them."

"I haven't heard that assessment," I admit. Racking my brain, I don't think I ever met the man in person. Just watched my father attend every gala. "He never made me attend that particular event though. Maybe he knew the irony as well?" I try to laugh, but the sound trickles out far too softly.

"Would it help if I were there?"

He makes it sound so simple. So casual.

"How would it look?" I wonder—without refusing outright. "If I show up with my father's archenemy? I might as well be dancing on his grave."

"We don't have to appear together, then," he suggests. "But I will be there. We both may have our own aims, but I will still be there. For you."

"Thank you—"

"Don't." He laughs in that dangerous way that churns my stomach. "Because I would like to request something in return *por favor.*"

"Oh?"

He lifts our clasped hands and brushes his mouth against the back of mine. There, he murmurs, "I want you to sleep here tonight."

"More sex?" I quirk my lips. "Isn't that already part of our arrangement?"

"You don't understand." He laughs, shaking his head, his thumb still stroking my palm. "I want you to sleep with me tonight. In my bed. I don't require sex, but…"

His deepening tone invokes a shiver I'm sure he senses.

"I want you naked," he admits. "Beneath my sheets. I want to be able to touch you. Hold you. All to better assess your fear of the dark, of course."

"And own it," I say, referring to his newest conquest. "Do you really think you're up to the task, Mr. Villa?"

There's a storm building on the horizon, evident in purplish clouds swarming the skyline.

"I'm willing to employ my…resources to attempt such an endeavor," he warns. "Though I have some work that must be done this afternoon."

"Work," I parrot. Disappointment unfurls in my chest before I can help it, erasing the tendrils of fire sowed by his words. "After all this time, I still don't know exactly what it is you do."

"*Sí.*" He releases my hand, bracing his on his knees. "Though I'm sure your father told you all about my career path."

"But I want to hear it from you." I reach for his hand again. It twitches as if he has to fight not to pull away. "I'm sure there's more to you than supposedly running a criminal empire and using art for money laundering purposes."

"Is there?" He tugs his hand free and stands, grabbing his cane propped against the end of the chaise. "I need to leave earlier than expected, it seems. I'll be back—"

"I've offended you." Even if I have no idea how. "I'm sorry if I did."

His footsteps slow and then increase as he approaches the door. "I'll return later tonight if you decide to humor my offer. *Adios.*"

I listen to the door close after him, unwilling to move from my slumped position. Already, the sunlight is fading, surrendering to a darkening skyline.

The muted color scheme of my surroundings works to enhance the ominous aura tainting the atmosphere. Alone again with my thoughts, I find it harder to ignore the most dangerous ones teasing the edges of my psyche.

My father.

He's dying.

He's lying.

And without him, I have no one. Damien Villa may be a fitting diversion now, but for how long will he stay? How long until I bore him? How long before I can no longer take the secrets evident between us even as all other boundaries fall?

How long before I break under the pressure of it all?

I shower and linger naked in the bathroom of my private suite. To Mr. Villa's credit, the décor is complementary to the scarlet and ebony hues of the bedroom itself. A large sunken tub with golden features and black marble flooring create a dark, luxurious oasis.

And a lonely one.

When I finally return to my room, I grab a robe and then creep into the hallway, inching toward that dangerous barrier that divides his half from mine. If one were to describe my assigned rooms, they might as a mocking array of posh socialite meets repressed exhibitionist—but his…

The hallway extends, opening onto a large, spacious room stocked only with an easel and a stool. Simplistic at first glance, but the atmosphere feels different in here than at his other studio. Dark walls and onyx stone flooring lend to a quieter space. Calmer. I imagine him painting something far different from the average nude muse while in here. A hint of what such subject may be reveals itself the farther I roam into the suite.

The next room contains a relatively simple bed draped in black sheets. But the walls…

Painted canvas covers nearly every inch of them. So many scenes are depicted that I wander aimlessly, observing every one.

They transport me. Into amber fields. Ochre skies. A riverbank. A sea of growing crops. Each scene is frozen in painstaking detail, creating a parallel universe fit to rival that of his greenhouse. Flowers are a tangible escape.

But in this room, he created one from memory.

Enthralled, I find myself sitting on the end of his mattress, lost in the clashing views. It's a strange thing to be inside someone's mind. To see the world how they do, even if it's via snippets. Fragments. Damien Villa may be blind now, but he hoarded his recollection of the sky. The various hues of blue. The golden kiss of sunlight. How many secrets lurk behind his blindfold?

Hours must pass as I try to ponder that very question. Eventually, I feel tired enough to risk lying down—but my eyes have barely closed when I hear it. Thunder shattering the silence. Lightning flashes, illuminating the room and throwing every shadow into stark relief.

I find myself lurching upright and pacing circles until I wind up retreating to the scarlet room, drawn by a faint, musical melody. My cell phone. It rings again as I fish it from my purse, battling another monstrous roar of thunder. I reach for it and find a call from an unknown number. Only God knows who it could be. I shouldn't answer, given the hell of this past week.

But when lightning strikes, my finger slips.

"Hello?"

"While I have kept your room free of surveillance, I feel it is only fair if I am allowed to monitor *my* private space." An amused voice, slightly accented, drips into my ear like liquid sin and a breath I didn't realize I was holding escapes in a gasp. "You were in my bed," he adds, lingering over the possessive term. "I'm disappointed you chose not to stay there."

"I…" I grit my teeth to keep from gasping again. "I thought you were in the middle of business, Mr. Villa—"

"I am," he says. In the background, I hear men's voices, discussing some unknown topic. "But when more important matters come across my radar, I must give them my full attention. I sincerely hope you enjoyed the comfort of the mattress. I fully intend to ensure you experience it thoroughly."

"If only you weren't so damn busy." I feign a strained sigh as thunder rumbles, sounding fainter compared to the tenor of his voice. More lightning flashes as if fighting for my attention. "I'm sure you'll be tied up for most of the night."

"Unfortunately, yes…" He sounds wary. Oh my, I wonder why.

"That's too bad," I exhale, distantly aware of rain lashing at the window. "If you were here, I'd let you help me experience the comfort of your bed firsthand."

"Oh?" His tone falls flat, suddenly cold. Maybe the change in demeanor has something to do with how heavily I'm breathing into the receiver? I'll hate myself for this later. I know I will.

But when he speaks, he's louder than thunder. Even whispered and hushed, his voice outlasts the rain. I'll take it over silence, and later, I'll lament over how pathetic that makes me.

"Yes. I'm sure we could give your precious mattress a thorough 'testing.' Maybe I'd even let you taste what I know you can't stop thinking about since the other night." God, did those words come from me? Apparently so.

Harsh, heavy breaths fan into the speaker, distorting all other noise. "Is that so?"

"*Sí.*" I try to mimic the sultry tones of his accent—a low grunt from his end is my reward. I roll onto my back, ignoring what my free hand does as I let it drift along my thigh—but my body's reaction betrays me. My breathing falters. Then quickens to match the suddenly rapid rate of his. "Very much so." My fingers make contact with sensitive flesh, which draws a moan from me that isn't faked. Isn't part of the game.

"Damn." His teeth clip the word. "I'm giving your proposal serious consideration."

"If only you were here…" Another brush of my finger over heated skin elicits another moan voiced into the speaker. Thunder. Flashing. Darkness. All of it threatens to ruin the facade even the illusion of his presence wraps me in. "I need you here—"

"Gentlemen." It takes my brain a second to realize that he's no longer speaking to me. "I'm terribly sorry. We'll have to reconvene at another date."

I hear muttered voices and shuffling of what sounds like furniture. Then his voice returns, aimed only toward me.

"You got your wish," he warns, sounding more as though he's promising my doom. "I'm on my way to collect in full what I'm owed."

I gasp. "You're joking—"

"Far from it, Ms. Thorne," he growls.

Which means he really just ended what sounded like a meeting for me. Because of sex. Even so, he doesn't hang up right away. I can tell he's moving. Quickly.

"I suggest you hurry, Mr. Villa." I'm not playing fair, but I'm beyond caring.

I'm warm instead of frozen for once. On fire instead of shivering. Thunder rumbles, but I feel damn near invincible instead of fearful. Lightning crackles, but I barely even hear it. Just the promise conveyed in every curse he mutters under his breath as my fingers stroke and my breaths quicken in response. It's unfair that he can do this to me.

"I can't stop thinking of how you felt inside me—"

"Son of a bitch." Rapid breathing stutters through the receiver. Is he running? The blaring sounds of traffic flood the background before I can be sure. Then the sound of a door opening. Slamming.

"I want you inside me like I've never needed anything else."

"Maddening woman." More cursing diminishes his usual polished persona. He sounds harsher now. Vulgar. "You don't know what you're—"

"I can't stop imagining how your tongue would feel on me."

Utter silence comes from his end and I know I've crossed a line from which there is no turning back.

I bite my own tongue, but it's no use. It's like he said. I'm fucking mad. "Tell me how it would feel."

He groans. "Like heaven, sweet girl. I'll show you."

My heart stutters at the promise. Hopeful. God, I'm going insane.

"I'll show you how badly I've craved your taste. And there…you're already moist for me, I bet. *Dios mío,* woman. I'll show you."

He doesn't whisper. His driver must hear him. And he doesn't care.

With every grated word, fingers stroke the tiny bundle of nerves that has me seeing stars. One. Two. A galaxy of them. "And then what?"

"*Mierda,*" he swears, his voice rasping. "I'll have you on your knees, *dulce niña.* You'll regret this little game."

But therein lies the joke. For the first time in so long, I'm not playing someone's game. The rules have been forgotten. I'm on an island unto myself. And with every uttered word, the further I remove myself from any hope of redemption.

"Damien," I whisper, dropping the pretense. My voice shakes and I squeeze my eyes shut against another startling flash of lightning. "I…need…you…here *now.*"

He bellows something, presumably to the driver amid a smattering of honking horns. Another door slams followed quickly by the delicate chime that sounds like that of an elevator arriving.

He never stops speaking to me. Harsh words too filthy to process—but the twisted promises aren't what makes my heartbeat stutter. All that matters is his tone. Thick. Gritty. Desperate.

Even the world's best actor couldn't fake the tremor in his voice.

Finally, I hear the door to the suite itself open and slam. I lurch upright, straining my ears to track the surge of footsteps marching toward my room.

Seconds later, a monster appears at the foot of my bed, dripping rainwater onto the floor. His hair fell out of its usual ponytail, his blindfold slightly askew.

"You don't even understand how important the meeting you derailed was." He laughs while shedding his coat, leaving it at his feet. "It will take months to rebuild those connections. Perhaps even years. And yet...I'm here—and not for sex," he clarifies, inching a step closer. "I could hear the tremor in your voice. I knew you were afraid—"

"No," I start to argue. "That's not why I wanted you—"

"I know." He nods, shrugging off the concern. "But I'm still here regardless."

And even he doesn't seem to know why.

Neither do I.

"You could always leave," I pitch halfheartedly, hating the hitch in my voice. "I'd hate to think I interrupted some massive criminal undertaking—"

"Come here." He crooks a single finger, beckoning me closer.

I shed the silken sheets and rise to my knees. Even from the slight distance, I see his nostrils flare, his tongue tracing his lower lip.

"*Dios mío,* I can smell you already," he growls, inviting with a crooked finger. "Now, sweet girl. Tonight, you show me firsthand how to touch you."

Heart hammering, I inch closer and he extends his hand, heavy palm upright. A tremor racks my spine as I lie back and guide him between my legs. I'm groaning before I even feel him. He cups me roughly and the friction negates the softness of his skin.

"Spread your legs for me. Wider—*sí,* like that." With every word, he flexes his hips, rubbing himself against me—but never inside. So close to what he promised.

It's torture. It's sin. I moan against him without a damn given for anyone who could overhear. Still, I let him set the pace. I let him control the intensity of sensation, barely fucking enough.

It's raw fire against tender flesh and all I can do is bite my tongue against the onslaught.

"No," he growls, easily maneuvering above me. "You let me hear you. You moan when I touch you." His thumb slips inside me, triggering an echo of what he craves. "And when I fuck you, sweet girl…you scream."

His knee nudges my legs farther apart, and he grips my hips, positioning me. The rasp of his undone zipper teases the air before I feel him. Taunting at first, sliding a pulsing ridge of flesh between my legs. Sinful, raw friction next. Nowhere near enough. Then, without warning, he thrusts hard. Deep. Strangled noise rips from my throat.

"Like that," he groans, rocking his hips to almost draw free before slamming back in. "*Mierda*, like that."

He bucks, thrusting deeper. Unhurried. Air thickens. The world fades. My hands clutch his shoulders. My knee curls, fighting for leverage against his thigh. His nearness triggers every memory from the other night. The soreness. The pleasure.

My brain is reduced to a senseless thought on an infinite loop: *Need more.*

He's trapping me in this memory, more vibrant than any painting hanging on his walls. I'll never forget the taste of him on my tongue. The words he growls into my ear as my breaths quicken and the tension building inside me overflows.

Afterward, I don't know how long we lie still, his arms around me, his mouth at the base of my throat. Clarity returns only as he shifts easing back as a disappointed pang shoots through my belly.

"I won't go far, sweet girl," he says thickly. Sure enough, he only snatches up one of the sheets kicked toward the bottom of the bed. "I may require your assistance," he says, a wry smile tilting his mouth, visible even in the dark.

I help him unfurl the blanket and he draws it around us both, resuming his previous position of holding me.

"You're shaking," he says, running his hand along my arm.

"It could be shock," I playfully counter. "I think I'm relaxed for once."

Despite everything. All I feel is his heat sheltering me from another storm raging beyond the confines of the suite.

"One day, I will take you south," he murmurs as his fingers creep up to my hair, sinking into the strands of it. "The storms there are fiercer, but the sound… Here, it's just loud, aimless noise, but there? Out in the country, it's like a symphony when it rains. The animals howl. The trees creak. You would never feel alone, of that I am sure."

A tired laugh escapes me, sinking into the sheets. "It sounds beautiful. Do you miss it there?"

"Sometimes…" He stops stroking me, but his arm tightens, drawing me farther against his chest. "Maybe in some ways I've stopped myself from going back—at least alone. Not because I fear the memories, but…"

"But?" I retaliate for the intimate way he's touching me by sliding one of my hands back to rest on his hip.

A low sound rumbles from his throat. "But I don't want to become the person I was when I lived there," he admits. "He was violent. Cold. He could do unspeakable things without hesitation. There was no poise…no patience. I've left that man behind and I've taken great pains to become someone else. Even if that someone is a reformed *'criminal mastermind who uses his paintings for money laundering.'"*

My lazy smile falls flat. "Tell me about it. I…I won't judge you," I add in a rush.

"It's not a part of my life I like to relive," he admits. A hitch disrupts his deep baritone—a rare, fleeting slip in his façade.

"But you know about my past," I say softly. "I want to know about yours."

"Fair enough." His heavy sigh bastes my skin in warm breath.

I inhale it, feeling that one wrong move may shatter the fragile trust he's willing to extend my way. "Start with where you grew up," I suggest.

"*Sí.* As I mentioned before, I was born in a small village in southern Colombia. My mother was an American missionary who came to the country on a mission trip, where she met my father. He was a farmer who seemed kind and respectable, at least at first."

"And then?" I prompt when he's fallen silent.

Muscles flex beneath his skin and I wince; he's holding me even tighter. "She quickly learned that he was not the man she thought he was. And that was the reality my brothers and I were born into."

"I'm sorry," I whisper.

He laughs. "Don't be. In some ways, I had a wonderful childhood. Children, after all, tend to be oblivious of such things. Violence becomes a rare, fleeting event in a world filled with lazy days running through the fields or swimming in the rivers. A bit like a thunderstorm, if you don't mind the comparison."

"It fits," I admit. "So why did you really leave?"

His lips flutter over my shoulder and I arch into the contact. Only now does he give me more.

"We grew up," he says simply. "And our father…he became worse. His usual methods of tyranny before then had been the average daily outburst. Striking my mother, or myself, or one of the others. But as we grew older, something in him changed. One night, he cornered our mother and accused her of eyeing another man. She hadn't, of course, but the truth didn't matter to him. In his madness, he decided that the only way to punish her was to ensure that her eyes could never stray again."

"No—" I stiffen, my breath caught in my throat. Admittedly, I haven't thought too much about his blindness —just the one snippet of information he's revealed before now: that he blinded himself.

"*Sí, dulce niña*," he murmurs into my skin, once again deploying his uncanny skill for reading my mind. "I confronted him, and he chose to punish me instead."

I close my eyes, imagining the horror of it. "And that's why you left?"

"Part of it," he admits. "I can tell from the dread in your voice what you're thinking—but don't. Do not pity me. In some ways, my…injury made me stronger. I don't take the beauty in life for granted. I capture it. Enhance it—or corrupt."

More specifically, he hordes it, trapping what entices him in paint and canvas. Even if he can't see them, he can relive what he lost in the act of painting. After all, I experienced firsthand how passionate he can be when it comes to his art.

"What happened next?"

"Despite my…sacrifice, my mother died not long after," he says. "I knew that, without her, my brothers and I needed to come to America—any way we could."

I fill in what the rumors about him claim. "Even via the drug trade."

He makes a low sound in his throat. Part laugh. Part groan. "Perhaps. Those desperate boys may have built a life using whatever skills they could. Pardon my evasiveness, but I am not used to baring my secrets in front of the daughter of a judge."

"You can trust me." I'm surprised by how earnest I sound. "I have my own share of secrets."

"Oh?" His fingers still over my hip.

"I told you that Diane gave me my father's will?"

He nods, leaning into me with every motion of his head. "*Sí.*"

"She wanted me to find whatever he left for me in a safety deposit box. I went alone."

"And?" If he's angry about the deception, I can't tell.

"I found an old note written from someone in the city's police department."

"Really?"

I stiffen at the sudden grit in his tone. Maybe he is angry after all.

"What did it say?"

"It doesn't really matter," I whisper. "The point is: It just proved something I didn't want to face."

"And what was that?" His tone softens just enough for the tension to leave my limbs.

In his arms, I feel brave enough to admit the truth I haven't faced. "When I read it, I...I hated him. Just for a second, but I felt it." Tears spill down my cheeks, but I don't bother to brush them away. "I hated him. Do you remember how Diane begged me to represent him at a benefit gala?"

He nods.

"Well, I haven't even picked out a dress or made arrangements. I'm not sure I can show my face to those people and pretend that everything is fine."

"And you don't have to. Trust your emotions. Do only what feels right."

"That's the problem," I admit. "I don't know what's real or not. I don't know what I should do—"

"I will tell you," Damien says, sweeping his hand along my thigh. "All you need to do now is sleep. In the morning, if you change your mind, I'll be there for you."

"Thank you," I whisper. "I mean it. Lately…it's like I can't feel anything anymore."

"Oh?" His fingers slip to graze my inner thigh. "I'm insulted, Ms. Thorne. You must be a damn good actress if you are incapable of feeling *anything*."

My moan betrays me as a liar, and then I inhale, fighting for clarity. "Outside of bed," I blurt. "Outside… Away from you."

He goes rigid. Just as doubt creeps in, he molds against me, cradling me in muscle and heat. "I am content to make you feel," he concedes. "For now."

"Oh?"

"One day, I will demand more. But we can save that discussion for another time. Just sleep for now, sweet girl. I don't want to tire you out too soon. Sleep."

And I find it easy to within his arms.

Even as the storm continues to rage around us.

THIRTEEN

ddly enough, I don't feel abandoned or insulted by the empty bed I've woken up to. Especially not when I roll over and find a bouquet of black roses where Damien last slept. I finger a single stalk and lower my nose to the petals flooding the air with their crisp perfume.

A smile lingers on my lips as I shower and get dressed in a plain gray dress—the closest thing to black in my wardrobe. While I brush my hair, I make a mental note to remind Damien to have my things brought over. Though it seems he's decided to ignore my wishes for now. Instead, I find a white box placed tauntingly in front of my door. It's wrapped in a bright-pink bow, dangerously inviting.

My fingers shake as I open it. Inside, I find yards of tulle and lace—a dress made of the thinnest beige lace imaginable. A skirt of tulle billows from the waist, but the only form of coverage the wearer might hope to find comes in the form of delicate silk appliqués sewn around the garment.

Flowers. Thousands of them, presumably affixed by hand, spanning nearly every color of bloom imaginable.

Score one Damien Villa. I can concede defeat in this round. I don't even know whether to add the dress to my closet or plant it. I briefly consider trying it on before I finally notice the envelope tucked inside the box.

Heyworth Thorne could only pray for such a representative, someone wrote in elegant script.

A kind, if bracing reminder of reality.

Returning to my room, I reach for my phone but find no new messages from Diane. By the time I arrive at the hospital, that familiar weight of dread returns, dragging on my limbs like a lead ball and chain.

I hesitate near the door for at least an hour, wringing my fingers to the point of pain. Finally, I step inside, steeling myself for whatever I might find.

"No change," Diane says tiredly as I approach.

Daddy's eyes are open, staring blankly even as she strokes her hand along his cheek.

"I'm going to go get some lunch, darling." She smothers a yawn into her palm and forces a smile. "Want anything?"

I shake my head and settle into the other chair pulled up to his bedside. For what feels like hours, I stroke the back of his hand, searching his empty eyes for any hint of life. God, there are so many questions I need to ask, but when I finally gather the nerve to voice one, all I can think to say is,

"Why?" My finger shakes, tracing the path of his cheek to no response. "Why, Daddy? Were you sent to find me for a reason? Was this all just some twisted game—just tell me why!"

"Is everything all right?"

I look over to find a nurse at the door, an eyebrow raised.

"I'm fine," I say, swiping at the tears welling in my eyes. "We're fine." Once she's gone, I admit, "I went to the safety deposit box," directing the words at my lifeless father. "I saw the page you had hidden there. But why? What is it you couldn't tell me?"

I wait—a folly that doesn't sink in until one of the machines monitoring his vitals shrieks, sounding an alarm. The nurse returns to fix it. Leaves again. And I laugh, shaking my head.

"I'm crazy." Sighing, I withdraw my hand and start to stand. "I'm going crazy—"

"Dead." The raspy voice echoes like a gunshot.

I jump, scanning the room for an intruder, but all I find is shadow. Shadow and…

A pale hand that lurches toward me, grasping mine so tightly that I gasp.

"D-Daddy?"

His cold, blue eyes turn to me, blinking. "Dead," he croaks again. "He's dead…he's dead. He's dead!"

More alarms go off from various machines and an army of nurses races into the room, scrambling to quiet them.

"I'm going to ask you to step outside, dear," one of them says, guiding me to the door.

Even in the hallway, I can hear him. Shouting. Screaming in an eerie refrain.

"He's dead!"

"*M*s. Thorne?" I jump as a woman in a lab coat appears at the mouth of the private lobby near the ICU. "Yes?" I scramble up from a couch, smoothing my hands along my rumpled dress. "How is he?"

"Stable for now," the woman says with a strained smile. "He's asking to see you. I would ask you try to limit tiring him out too soon, but you're free to see him."

I follow her into the hall, my heart in my throat. Before I even enter the room, I can sense a shift in the atmosphere. The air isn't so heavy. Someone opened a window, allowing in a fresh breeze, as well as turned on the main light in the room. Bathed in the yellow glow, Daddy is lying in bed, propped up by a wall of pillows. His frail hands settle together over his lap, but his eyes…

They tiredly focus on me as I approach.

I falter and brace my hand over my chest. "D-Daddy?"

"Sweet pea." His thin, frail voice barely rises above a whisper—but my heart throbs at the sound. I never thought I'd hear it again.

"How are you feeling?" I take up a chair beside his bed and grasp one of his hands.

He squeezes once reassuringly, and despite everything, a smile tugs on my lips. Though I can't prevent a tear from escaping, sliding down my cheek.

"I've been better," he says with a weak laugh.

"I was worried about you," I admit, swiping at my face with the back of my hand. "We *all* were. Diane should be here soon. She got stuck in traffic—"

"I'm sorry, Juliana." He brushes his other hand along my cheek. "I'm so, so sorry."

"We don't have to talk about that now." I force a smile and fiddle with his blankets, smoothing them. "We just need to focus on your health—"

"I've lied to you." His reedy, broken voice sounds nothing like the confident man I know, and a panicked part of me isn't ready to have that image of him I've held for so long tarnished.

"Daddy, please. We don't need to talk about that now—"

"I've lied to you," he insists, his eyes watering. "All this time… I'm so sorry."

"Then just… Just tell me why."

It's strange. I've never begged him for anything before. Not the most coveted Christmas presents, or the chance to stay up even a minute past my bedtime. I accepted his rules and cherished whatever he desired to give me. Based on that simple trust, I love him more than I've ever loved anyone.

Or so I thought.

The same way I thought he loved me. That my adoption had been the whim of a kindhearted soul and not an act of greed. God, I need to believe those lies more than ever. But they're slipping away from me like tabloid fodder printed on cheap paper.

"You have every right to hate me." His fingers flex in mine as he stares into my eyes. They're bloodshot and hurt to keep open for too long. Or maybe it's his face that stings my vision and makes my eyelids lower. "I don't blame you, sweet pea. In some ways, I hate myself for what I've done. There is no excuse."

"You knew who he was," I say thickly. "The man who attacked me. All this time and you knew."

"Juliana…" His face pales. Artificial light enhances the wrinkles and he ages decades in seconds, becoming a wizened old man I barely recognize. "I refuse to lie to you again." He releases my hand as if burned. "It's true."

I wince as that hollow feeling inside of my chest festers and spreads like cancer. *Truth*…that twenty years ago,

Heyworth Thorne defended a man accused of murder before he ever sat on a judge's bench.

And the man in question?

"Who?" My words run together, slurred with tears and pain. "Just tell me who he is please!"

All those years of therapy after Leslie's death. The grim insinuation that maybe I had something to do with her murder. The agonizing years the Matodas have gone without closure.

All of it congeals into a painful ball weighing on my chest.

"Is that why you adopted me?" I add hoarsely when he hasn't replied. "Guilt?"

"Perhaps," he admits. "Or greed. I knew I'd been used. I wanted to right that wrong—any way I could. Even if it meant using a little girl by taking guardianship over her so that if the moment came…I could give authority for her to testify."

"That's why you adopted me?"

He doesn't deny it. The man I've thought of as my father simply lowers his head, his features agonized. "I knew what I'd done. And I thought if I could get you to the right officer who could ask the right questions, we could bring him down for good. But then I met you. This sweet, innocent girl… Call me whatever you want, Juliana, but don't you doubt for a second that I love you. Too much, some might say. And they *have* said." He blinks, sending moisture dripping down his cheeks. "In the end, I couldn't bear to put you on the stand. I knew what that would do to you—"

"Don't use me as your excuse." I replay those early days over and over in my mind. All those birthdays of playing cat-and-mouse with Simon. All those nights wasted fearing my unseen boogeyman. Another terror takes hold, impossible to swat aside this time. "Did you give him access to me?" I can't even look at him.

"Never," he swears in a tone I've never heard him use before. "I would never let that monster near you! I made sure, even when I—" He breaks off, coughing.

"Daddy?" I draw back, lurching to my feet. "You need rest. I should go—"

"No!" He grabs my hand with a strength that contradicts his frail appearance. I doubt I could pull away if I tried, so I sit. "Everything I've done has always been to protect you. Maybe not as well as I should have," he admits. "But at least you'll never have to worry about that monster again."

Twisted hope and dread form an anvil that crushes my lungs. Gasping, I choke out, "Who is he?"

"I can't tell you his name. I think it would confuse you more and I need to explain." Pain distorts his pale features. "Just trust me when I tell you that he's dead. Has been for four years now. He will never hurt you again."

I recoil, frowning. "Dead? N-No. That's wrong—"

"He's dead," my father insists. "I saw the bastard lowered into his grave myself. I spent so damn long watching him. Waiting for one shred of—"

"Heyworth!" Diane appears breathless in the doorway, one of her hands braced against her chest. "Heyworth!"

They scan each other, their eyes brimming with tears, and I don't have the heart to ruin the moment by dredging up the past. Not now, when I can barely form a coherent thought. *Four years.* My mind keeps replaying those words over and over.

"I'll leave you two alone," I croak, standing.

"I know the gala is tonight darling," Diane starts, "but I may be late—"

"Stay here."

"I'm sorry, sweet pea," Daddy calls after me, his voice broken and hoarse. "I'm so, so sorry."

Because he's lying to me, I decide as I race into the hall. He has to be. Because if Simon died four years ago…

Only one man in the world has the means and knowledge to replace him.

Someone worse than a monster.

FOURTEEN

I don't know how I've made it back to Damien's without breaking apart. Screaming. Instead, I'm dead silent during the ascent to his suite. Numb. With my thoughts in turmoil, I enter the foyer and find a note waiting for me on the end table instead of the man himself.

I'll meet you there tonight, it reads. *Do wear the dress.*

His dress: a beautiful, mocking confection of a betrayal too cruel to fathom. A strangled sound creeps from my throat and I'm on my knees, my eyes streaming. Somehow, I manage to smother any sound against my palm and stand. On trembling legs, I enter my scarlet room. Here, I pull my new dress on, but I don't even recognize the stranger staring back at me from the mirror's surface.

Her hollow eyes stare blankly ahead, no less soulless than one of Sampson's eerie paintings. All I need is a sea of flowers to drown in and the irony would be complete.

When I enter the hall hours later, Julio is there to usher me into a waiting car, and I arrive at the gala to find a crowd hounding the few patrons brave enough to enter the building through the throng.

"We can go around, miss," Julio suggests, but I shake my head and push the door on my end open.

Every year, the Wellington family throws the event at the same mansion on the outskirts of the city. The modern design serves as the perfect backdrop to the mixture of old money and hopeful delegates arriving by the carful.

It's the perfect setting to face my past.

A perfect setting to accept the truth: I was only ever of use to anyone as one thing.

A token. A pawn. A piece in a game.

"Juliana!" a reporter shouts, startling me back to the present. "Is it true that your father's health is in stable condition?"

"Allow me," a man cuts in.

I turn and find someone looming behind me, cutting a striking figure in a tailored black suit.

"May I?" He takes my arm and guides me forward.

Despite the crush of reporters, we enter the venue unmolested. In the foyer, Harrison helps me out of my coat and tosses it to a nearby attendant.

"I'm surprised you came," he says, raking his gaze over me. "Rumor has it that you weren't particularly fond of your father's return to politics in the first place. And this event…

Gerald Wellington was a man even your father despised, though he was more than willing to take his money."

"I've always supported my father publicly," I croak. "Always."

"I heard he's awake." Stepping forward, he leads me past an army of valets laden with trays of wine ready to be served to the partygoers. "One might presume you'd be with him."

"He wanted me here." God, I hate how my voice keeps breaking. Maybe the will didn't cement it, but just being here does. I am Heyworth Thorne's daughter for better or for worse. He lied to me; there's no erasing that. But at the end of the day, he still trusts me with his most important possession of all: his name. "I'm doing this for *him*."

"Well, perhaps you may be interested in lending his support in the form of an endorsement?"

"An endorsement?" I raise an eyebrow, scanning the ballroom for a familiar face in a sea of beautiful strangers. A few weeks of self-imposed exile and I barely recognize the polished upper crust of society anymore. I'm a tainted doll now with visible cracks, drawing eyes everywhere I go.

"Yes. In light of Heyworth's unfortunate health concerns, my son Kyle has decided to run for mayor in his stead." He nods toward a man standing near a corner of the room, surrounded by fawning guests. At a glance, a slight resemblance is obvious in their confident stature and dark-brown hair. "An endorsement from you in your father's place would be a fitting show of solidarity."

"I appreciate the offer," I say, forcing a smile. "But I should discuss it with him first."

"He's talking?" His head swivels in my direction, his eyebrows furrowed. "His condition has improved that much?"

"It's better than expected," I admit, blinking tears back. "But still touch and go."

"I see." He lowers his head, his eyes downcast. "I'm sorry to hear the old son of a bitch still isn't at his full health. Maybe I should schedule another visit? See if he knows anything about what may have caused his condition?"

"Maybe…" I trail off as a figure near the back of the room catches my attention.

A man standing tall, his eyes shielded by a blindfold. Whether he realizes it or not, women flock to him, casting him searching glances.

From them, he might choose his next willing muse.

His next victim to destroy.

"Excuse me, Juliana," Harrison says, releasing my arm. "I'm sorry to abandon you, but I think I see a colleague."

Abandon. The word stings more than the context—turning into agony the more I observe the blindfolded figure across the room. His head is cocked and I imagine him intently listening to every bit of conversation around him, discerning more through observation than I figure most could ever see at one time.

Like the fact that I'm the center of attention. Several pairs of eyes dart in my direction, scanning the daring cut of my gown. I copy them, eyeing the dress as if for the first time. As odd as it feels to suspect, I can't shake the feeling that he created this. Designed it, maybe. It's too damn intricate. A risqué play on fashion only a true artist would dare attempt. Jaw-droppingly sheer fabric and strategically placed appliqués to shield my nipples and waistline from view. At the same time, it's matronly in shape, with a high neckline and a formfitting bodice. I catch several photographers pointing their camera in my direction, and I suspect I'll make tomorrow's society pages.

"I was wrong," someone murmurs heatedly into my ear.

I look over at the corner; the secluded figure has vanished.

"I knew the dress would look stunning on you," the man in question admits into my ear, sliding his hand over my lower back. "But given the reaction tonight, *mierda*… I almost wish I could see it myself."

The world seems to think so. As if on cue, I catch several murmured compliments directed my way.

You look beautiful.

You look marvelous.

What a stunning dress.

Pretty statements that merely skim the surface. How I look, never how I feel. To them, I'm just the same old Juliana with a different coat of paint. But therein lies the real question. Who is the woman they've known all along?

And who is the man by my side?

"I need to talk to you," I croak.

"*Sí.* And I need to talk to you." He extends his cane, deploying it like a sensor to ensure he doesn't come close to anyone else. "Though, as promised, I will ensure we aren't seen together for long. When you are ready, head to the restroom, *¿sí?*"

He pulls away and I watch him go, my heart in my throat. There's nothing left to do but simper, and smile, and mingle.

It's nearly an hour before I escape into the bathroom, but Damien isn't lurking inside the stalls. Shaking, I claim a sink for myself and splash cold water on my face. Looking at my reflection, I try to see the same woman everyone else is. But I don't. I see a fraud in a dress that fits her too perfectly. Silk roses cup her breasts but threaten to expose her with the slightest shift of fabric. The entire construction is an elaborate dance between elegant and obscene.

Looking at myself, I settle my suspicion once and for all: He designed this. Only a madman could taunt me in the form of couture. Only Damien Villa could design a trap in the form of a dress.

And only he would be cunning enough to masquerade as a monster.

When Damien doesn't appear, I exit the restroom.

"Excuse me. Ms. Thorne?"

I turn and find a man approaching me. Tall and imposing, he cuts a striking figure almost as chilling as Damien. A name comes to mind as I meet his gaze. Kyle Harrison. He shares the same, piercing gaze as his father, honed like a laser.

"I hope my father spoke to you," he says while reaching for my hand. I shiver as he grasps my fingers, lifting them to his mouth, "I would love an endorsement from your father, even with his…current issues."

He smiles.

I cringe. "I appreciate the sentiment, but I'm not sure if—"

"Think on it," he urges, releasing me. "I would hate to see his legacy end in ruin."

I watch him go, so lost in thought that I nearly collide with someone walking past me. A giggling woman who staggers to regain her balance. Not that she seems to mind. "Are you Juliana?" she asks, her voice breathy.

When I nod, she steers the train of her navy-blue gown with one hand while offering me a white envelope in the other.

"A man asked me to give this to you." Her raised eyebrow indicates curiosity, but the wine on her breath leads me to believe she won't remember enough of this encounter to gossip about it later.

"Thank you." I take the note and watch her stumble into the restroom. Then I rip it open and read while hunched against the wall.

Come to the east wing.

The sender didn't even bother to sign it—not that he needed to. I can smell him. Sin and malice embedded within the paper itself.

Heart in my throat, I head further down the hall and slip from the ballroom altogether. The east wing is a simple trip across the foyer, but a man is standing guard near the archway leading toward it. My footsteps slow as I approach him, but he merely nods, allowing me to pass unaccosted.

It's dark. The winding hallway is illuminated only by the moonlight drifting in through beautiful antique windows that display a view of a private garden. Once I reach the ballroom, I have a crystal-clear view of the man responsible for this game of hide-and-seek. He's near a window, and bathed solely in the glow of moonlight, he's breathtaking.

"How do you like the dress?" he wonders, his voice easily reaching me.

I flinch. I'll never understand how he can make me feel more exposed than I did in a room with hundreds of people watching my every move. He doesn't just skim the surface. He has his head cocked so that his ears are in the prime position to capture every slow, unsteady breath I take. My deliberate footsteps.

"It's lovely," I say robotically, stopping short.

"Only for you… Is something wrong?"

I can't remember how to move until he beckons me with a crook of his finger and a challenging tilt of his chin.

"You're awfully quiet tonight."

The moment I'm close enough, he reaches out to decipher me through heated fingertips. Tasting me with a slow flick of his tongue along his lower lip. He breathes me in, analyzing my every action, and I stand there until he delivers his assessment.

"I designed this damn thing with you in mind," he admits, his voice quickly losing its polished cadence. He sounds guttural. Raw. Too damn honest. "I knew you'd wear it—"

"I feel overdressed," I counter, fighting to breathe.

"Oh?" He's scowling now. "It appears as though you're the talk of the ball. I could hear those bastards simpering from here. Though it seems none of them have noticed that, beneath this"—he swipes a teasing handful of fabric—"you're wearing nothing at all. How scandalous, Ms. Thorne."

I wrench away from him and cross my arms over my chest. One touch and he senses what a room full of people overlook. "Sometimes it feels like you know me better than I know myself," I whisper, my eyes burning. "*Too* well…"

"Oh?" His steps cease their slow advance. "I'm sensing that isn't a compliment."

I close my eyes, remembering the first time I saw his artwork at his gallery. That room where all those paintings of other women watched me. Now, their dead, blank stares take on a taunting aura, their gazes smug. *You fell for it,* they tell me. *Stupid, foolish bitch.*

"Have you been lying to me all this time?" I whisper brokenly. "About my father? ...Simon?"

"Juliana." His voice is deeper than before. Like he already knows damn well what I'm thinking. That he won't deny it. That he can't. "Talk to me," he commands. "What did you learn that is making you ask this?"

What did I learn? "The truth. That *you* were Simon."

It sounds insane out loud. Four years. Four years of torment. Of misery. Of lies, and pain, and memories...

But the more I relive every tortured moment, the more it makes sense. Only a man with such an intimate grip on my life could utterly control it.

And only an artist would relish in my misery.

"The real man has been dead for four years, according to my father. But you... You studied me," I say brokenly. "You studied *him*, and for four years, you've played his game."

"It's not what you think." He takes a step toward me, but I flinch back.

"Isn't it?" I force a callous laugh, but pretending doesn't help me now. Nothing. Turns. Off. The. Pain.

If anything, it grows, swelling into an agonizing lump in the pit of my stomach. Without giving a damn for decency, I double over. A gag racks my throat and vomit spills onto the floor. Noisily. Messily. I let him hear what the truth does to me. It destroys me. I'm brought to my knees by the force of it, robbed of even the voice to scream.

"I won't deny it," he says like it matters, still paces away. "But I won't hide the rest from you, either. You deserve to know the full truth."

More?

"I didn't leave the gifts for you to find—but," he adds before hope can even take root in my chest, "I know who did, at least vaguely though not a true identity. In some ways, I facilitated their actions, if only out of curiosity. I knew they upset you. I didn't know why—but upsetting you was enough."

"Because you had leverage," I whisper, seeing things how someone like him would: through a lens of hate and revenge. "Over my father. Over me."

That's how his world works, a muted landscape of give and take. Of death and decay. He doesn't admire flowers for their beauty—it's for their fragility, a reminder of the cruel balance he lives by.

"Why would I intervene in the life of the daughter of a monster like Heyworth Thorne?" he wonders. "It was more advantageous to me if I sat back and watched. I gathered what information I could use to my benefit, but your safety was not of my concern. I will admit that."

"So who is he?" I demand, swiping at my mouth. "Will you tell me that much?" But I'm not even surprised when he shakes his head.

If anything, he knows how to inflict pain with ruthless precision. "I have my suspicions, but the perpetrator is more powerful than I gave them credit for. They never used the same thug to plant your gifts." He pauses, waiting for that revelation to land.

And it does. Like a gut-punch.

"W-What do you mean?"

"They used hired experts, but never the same one twice. When questioned, the men couldn't name who hired them —and trust me, I was very *persuasive* in my questioning. The one night I finally did try to intercede, they ceased their little façade entirely."

"That's why I never got the fourth present," I say, ignoring the rest of his statement.

"There's more. I think whoever is responsible sent the attacker after you. The man with the knife."

My hand flies to my shoulder, tracing a healed wound through the fabric of my clothing. "The man who cut me at the hotel? And you never said anything?" I rasp. "Why?

"I had a hunch who it might be, but they are proving harder to nail down, just like your 'Simon.' Perhaps they are one and the same? But the more evidence I could use against them, the easier it would be to assert my influence when I finally unmask them."

"Even if they killed me?" I remember the fear. The isolation. The desperation. "You didn't help me. You let him…"

The world spins and I stagger to the wall, bracing my hands over it. It takes everything I have just to stay upright. To breathe.

"You let him hurt me," I choke out. "You left me alone—"

"I didn't know in advance or I would have stopped it," he swears. "But I won't make excuses. I should have told you." His tone is so different from the man who has comforted me during thunderstorms. This time, he doesn't smooth my hair or comfort me. He doesn't lend his presence like an anchor against the darkness clawing its way into my mind. He's the lightning rod for despair, incapable of understanding human suffering. So he merely watches me break. "I know nothing I can say could earn your forgiveness—"

"Forgiveness?" A broken laugh trickles out of me as I put the remaining pieces together.

Simon's sudden absence. The roses. *Roses are not your flower,* he said to me during our first true conversation. That was because he'd stolen it. He'd corrupted it.

Feeling sick, I tear at my neck, ripping his necklace from it. When the delicate pearl strikes the wall, I feel no satisfaction. Just pain. Maybe in his own twisted logic, he tried to tell me the truth all along. Oleander and roses. Poison and Simon's favorite gift.

"I...I thought I could trust you—no." I close my eyes and confess in a rush, "I did trust you. I *trusted* you."

It sounds so pathetic now. Trust a man so incapable of simple human emotion.

"I didn't want you to learn this way," he says, toying with me yet again. "Come with me. I can explain—"

"No!" I use the wall for leverage to steady myself. Then I run, stumbling for balance on jellied knees.

He doesn't try to stop me.

He doesn't spout any more lies about trust.

He lets me go without a word, and I leave a trail of tears like blood.

FIFTEEN

$\mathcal{A}$ stern-faced driver chauffeurs me to the hospital, but something feels different even before I step foot onto my father's floor, still wearing Damien's elegant creation.

"Miss?" A uniformed officer blocks my path as the elevator doors part. The gun prominent on his hip catches my notice first, his strained expression second. "I'm going to need to see some identification," he demands, extending his hand.

I fish through my purse for my ID. Eyeing it, the man deepens his frown. "Ms. Thorne? I'm going to need you to come with me."

"Is something wrong?" I ask. Alarm lances down my spine as I notice other officers clustered in the portion of the hall near my father's room. From here, the staticky noise issuing from their handsets creates an ominous hum.

"This way," the officer in front of me urges, but rather than lead me to my father's room, he takes me inside a small sitting room instead. "I'm going to ask you to sit, Ms. Thorne."

My heart lurches to my throat as I comply. "Please tell me what's going on."

"Your father is in serious condition," the officer says. "It seems as if there may have been foul play involved—"

"Foul play?" Panic sends sweat drenching my palms. "Like how?"

The man frowns and fishes something from his pocket. A notebook. Flipping it open to the first page, he says, "Have you ever heard of a shrub called oleander? Do you know anyone who might keep it potted or grow it?"

Grow…

It's like my brain disconnects from my body. I can see the world drift in and out of focus, but I have no control over my limbs. Trembling legs rob me of balance, and the man has to grab my arm, grunting in concern.

"Ms. Thorne?" When I don't answer, he adds, "We have reason to believe your father may have been poisoned. If you have any information, we request that you make a formal statement…"

He says something else, but the words meld into a frantic hum, drowned out by my heartbeat. I can't even see him anymore, just white flowers tucked carefully within a small pot, proudly displayed on my kitchen counter.

God, it's like I can hear him.

Dulce niña, did you really believe I wanted more than the obvious?

You meant nothing to me...

Just a means to an end.

And I always get what I want from those with something I desire.

"Juliana?"

I groan at the insistent voice—so distant yet so close, murmured inches from my ear. At least I think so...

My brain is a sluggish collection of thoughts, barely discernible. Groaning again, I try to make sense of anything. My body. My sanity. Gradually, I remember how to force my eyes open and the world comes into focus via blurred, broken snippets glimpsed from behind heavy eyelids.

A room. White walls. A haggard, worried face wearing an expression so pained that it makes my heart throb.

"Juliana," the woman says, her blond hair framing her angular face and her sunken cheeks. Diane. "Darling, can you hear me?"

I try and fail to nod, but my attempt must come across anyway, because she sighs, raking her trembling hands through her hair.

"Thank God. I was so worried. They had to sedate you, sweetheart."

"S-Sedate," I echo in a rasp. The word triggers an avalanche of memories.

Screaming. Crying. A nurse shoving a needle into my arm, her voice resolutely calm.

"You need to calm down, Ms. Thorne."

What a cruel dare. One I have no hope of obeying.

Because my father was nearly murdered—at least twice. And the man responsible used me to do so.

Even worse? He's taunted me with the murder weapon all along.

How long? I wonder, closing my eyes again as moisture seeps from them regardless. *How long was he watching? Waiting?*

"Where am I?" I ask if only to keep from sinking into the myriad of paranoid suspicions.

"Safe, darling." Diane smooths her hands along my hair, brushing strands from my face. "A private sitting room. Here."

Something cool brushes my lips, urging them to part. When I do, cool liquid drips between them. Water.

"Any better?" she asks.

I open my eyes again, this time taking in the narrow space surrounding us. Small. White walls and simplistic furniture. The kind of room dramas and sitcoms have made synonymous with stern doctors issuing bad news.

"Is he dead?" I whisper. God, I can't even look at her. My eyes burn, blurring and unfocused. Bile rises in my throat, blocking any other sound I could make. I can't stop seeing his face. Those eyes. His voice.

I love you, Juliana…

"He's stable," Diane says, her fingers stilling against my forehead. "Chief Harrison has personally overseen his case. He will find out who did this."

But I know who. My lips freeze, refusing to say it out loud. Almost as if that simple denial can prevent the fact from being final.

"Can I see him? My father?"

"Not yet, darling," Diane says. Her reddened eyes brim with tears even as she forces a smile. "He's still in the ICU—" She breaks off, staring beyond me, her lips clenched tight. "I'm so scared, honey. I'm so, so scared."

"Me too." I grab her hand, squeezing with reassurance.

Together, we sit in silence, separated from the chaos of the hall.

The smell draws me awake. Sharp and crisp. Familiar? My nostrils flare, identifying the traces of a masculine scent—but a different breed from the rich aroma tainting Damien. Cigar smoke. I swear I've smelled it before. It's harsh, evoking images of a stuffy bar or enclosed space. Secretive. The footsteps approaching me are heavier than Mr. Villa's as well, but in a way that conveys something more potent than mere confidence. It's arrogance.

Before I even open my eyes, a face appears in my thoughts and I name the figure out loud. "Chief Harrison."

"Morning, Juliana," he replies, his tone soft—for Diane's benefit, I realize. She's snoring, slumped onto the couch beside me. "I hope you don't mind if I ask you some questions?"

I stand, smoothing a hand over my wrinkled, stale dress. It's a gray one of Diane's, borrowed in place of the ball gown lying crumpled in a corner. "Of course."

"This way, then." He inclines his head.

I follow him into the hall. It's quiet, presumably early in the morning. Apart from a few scattered doctors and nurses, the main occupants of the hallway are wearing matching blue uniforms and sporting guns on their hips. His officers.

"I'm sure you've already heard what the doctors believe may be the cause of Heyworth's decline," Harrison starts, casting a glance toward my slightly sore arm. "I'm afraid to admit that we don't currently have any suspects. I have to ask… Do you have any idea where your father could come across something like oleander?"

A hard swallow contracts my throat as I find myself eyeing a section of wall across from us, cluttered with cheerful signs and reminders of hygiene. One sign in particular catches my interest: a bright-blue one urging any visitor to avoid visiting while experiencing a list of symptoms. Coughing. Sneezing. Fever. Pain.

The human body is apparently unoriginal in expressing when something is wrong. Right now, my throat is on fire, my lungs burning, my muscles throbbing. I lick my lips, ready to say it out loud, that terrible, horrible thing. It should be easy too. My only suspicion.

The obvious suspicion.

"No," I hear myself rasp. "I don't think they even grew the shrub at the house."

"Interesting." Harrison cocks his head, his dark eyes unreadable. They trace the contours of my face, settling over my trembling lips. They give me away, betraying all the things I can't seem to voice. Like the fact that I'm lying. "And you can think of no one with access to something like that? Someone who may want to hurt him?"

Pain lances through my heart as remnants of an accented voice whisper across my brain. *Do you really think I would hurt him, knowing how much he means to you?*

"N-No." I shake my head. "I'm sorry. I can't think of anything."

Harrison frowns, running his fingers along his jaw. "I'm disappointed, Juliana. If anyone could give insight into your father's health, I thought it might be you. You two were so close."

I flinch. Any other moment, I'd write off the pointed grit in his tone as paranoia. Exhaustion. Emotional distress. Taking a step back, I observe the man again. There's nothing untoward in his posture. Even his expression conveys concern. Too much concern.

"Let me give you my card," he says, reaching into his breast pocket for one. He extends it to me, meeting my gaze directly. "If you can think of anything at all, please don't hesitate—"

"If you had a suspect, would it even matter what I thought?" I ask, running my tongue along my dry, cracked lips. "You probably have the evidence—"

"Witness testimony *is* key evidence," Harrison corrects. "Sometimes in cases like this, it's the eye-witness account that clenches a verdict more than any piece of evidence. In fact, your father knew that better than anyone."

"K-Knew?" I echo. "Diane said his condition is stable. He should recover. Unless you've heard differently—"

"Of course." The man sighs and stares in the opposite direction. His hand captures his jaw as his thumb strokes the stubble growing there. "But in cases like this, who knows how quickly things may change? After all, as long as your father's attacker is still out there, he could try again."

"That's what your men are here for," I surmise cautiously. "To prevent that from happening."

"Of course." He nods and inclines his head. "But I will let you in on a secret, one that isn't very PC. My men are diligent, but they are human, and your father has some powerful enemies. Who knows what methods of deception they are capable of using if killing Heyworth Thorne is the ultimate goal?"

It feels like too pointed a statement to serve as general advice. Paranoia, I tell myself for the second time.

"I would hate for his condition to worsen," Harrison reiterates. "Which is why it is imperative that you tell me of any information that can help. Anything at all."

"I..." Motion catches my eye before I can finish the statement: another officer walking by, slim and pale. Familiar. The man who canvassed my apartment the other day.

"I have my men on him around the clock," Harrison explains as the man marches past my father's room. "Don't worry. He's in good hands."

"You've known him for a while, my father," I say. "Do you know anything about my case?"

He strokes his chin with the pad of his thumb. "The Borgetta case?"

"No." I shake my head while watching his reaction for any subtle shift. "*My* case. Leslie Matoda's case?"

And in some ways, Heyworth Thorne's case.

"My knowledge is a bit rusty on that front," he admits, shrugging. "I know they never caught the guy. He must have been quite the powerful man to avoid detection for so long. Or perhaps one with very powerful friends." He laughs, but there is no warmth in it. "I admire your strength to have survived such an ordeal. Even with your scars."

His gaze darts to my hip and I subconsciously run my fingers over my thigh, my cheeks heating. Did Daddy mention my old injuries to him?

"I'm sorry if discussing this upsets you," he says. "I know it was never closed."

"He wasn't caught," I admit thickly. "But… Hypothetically speaking, what if there was no real evidence? Just the word of a traumatized little girl. A girl in the crosshairs of a powerful monster."

A girl who someone in *his* department put on Heyworth Thorne's radar decades ago.

He sighs. "Some might say nothing would matter without hard evidence." Despite his blank expression, his tone hardens, a muscle in his jaw twitching. "Others…might suggest that a little girl's testimony, no matter how fragmented, could have an impact on a jury's ultimate decision. That, all discussions of her trauma aside, she would have to testify."

"And if she couldn't?"

"Couldn't?" A harsh sound escapes his throat. "Pardon my bluntness, Juliana, but what would matter more? The police doing their duty by putting a monster behind bars or one little girl's psyche?"

The answer is obvious. Painfully so, even. But one man may have seen it differently.

He may have felt so protective of one little girl, so involved in her trauma, that the mere hope of putting a monster away might not outweigh the damage of forcing her to stand alone. Forcing her to relive the same night over and over. Forcing her to face that man without true certainty her words would matter.

Such a man might grow overly protective of said little girl. Not because she was a pawn to use at his disposal, but because he loved her more than anything. Even his cherished version of justice.

"I'm sorry, Juliana." Harrison waves something white beneath my nose. A handkerchief. "I didn't mean to upset you."

"You haven't," I insist. But I accept the handkerchief regardless, swiping at my eyes with the delicate fabric. "It's been a stressful few days. That's all."

"I can imagine," he agrees. "Your father was awake. It would be rude of me to pry, but I can only assume that he didn't mention anything that may help to track down his attacker?"

"No," I say. "He… He just told me to be careful of who I trust. In this world, who can you really?"

"So cynical," Harrison scolds. "Your father was always a cautious man. Cautious, pragmatic, but sometimes to his detriment."

Something in how he said that phrase resonates in my bones, lingering even as he steps away from me, heading in the direction of his men.

"I'll let you rest in peace," he says. "But I'll be waiting for a call from you. Oh, and, Juliana?" He pauses, his head tilted expectantly, demanding a reply.

"Yes?"

"Heyworth and I may have had our differences, but I'm sure there is one point we both would agree upon: your safety." Again, he waits, almost as if daring me to question.

"My safety?"

"Yes. I've taken the liberty of stationing my men near your suite at the Lariat as well as here at the hospital. Any visitors will be logged and searched, and any move you make, even if it's a quick trip to the bathroom, you will be accompanied by one of my men. I want you to feel protected—"

"That's not necessary," I start to say, but he raises his hand, cutting me off.

"Oh, I believe it is entirely necessary. After all, you are Heyworth's most prized possession. I'd like him to know, if and when he recovers, that your life was in my hands. Have a good day, Juliana."

"Miss?" Another officer appears by my side. "Chief Harrison requests that you stay close by. We'll be positioned just outside if you need anything. Just ask."

"Thank you," I say, forcing a smile. The moment I slip inside the sitting room, my shoulders slump. Ice sinks into my spine, solidifying it as an uneasy dread builds in my belly. Paranoia, I tell myself over and over. Reckless paranoia.

Or perhaps, amid all his lies, Damien Villa uttered one semblance of the truth: *Trust your emotions.*

It's nearly the evening when another officer pokes his head through the doorway of the sitting room. "Good evening, ma'am. Can I get you anything?"

The question sounds harmless enough on its face. If only the man weren't wearing a uniform obviously a size too big. A Spanish accent colors his words as well—not particularly unusual for the city PD—but his eyes convey anything but the stern professionalism of Harrison's men. They shift, darting pointedly to the doorway.

"Is everything all right?" Diane murmurs sleepily, stirring beside me.

"Yes. Go back to sleep." I reassuringly run my finger along her back before standing, creeping toward the doorway for reasons I can't explain. Has life with Damien Villa corrupted me so thoroughly that I see deception and subterfuge no matter where I go? I'm almost convinced, until the officer leans in the moment I draw close enough.

"Vending machines are that way," he tells me, nodding down the length of the hall. This time of night, fewer officers linger, positioned at random intervals—but their mere presence reinforces Harrison's subtle boast. My "safety" is in his hands.

"Ms. Thorne?" The officer indicates in his chosen direction more strongly, gesturing with a wave.

I follow warily. When I reach the curve in the corridor, I don't find a vending machine. Just a hand reaching from nowhere to clench my arm and drag me into a vacant room.

"Easy," someone murmurs near my ear, their accent familiar. "Mr. Villa sent me. I'm a neutral party, merely here to see if you are all right."

"Neutral?" I whisper, turning to face the hulking figure behind me.

Julio. He's wearing his typical dark, nondescript suit and standing near the doorway of this empty hospital room.

Seeing him brings it all back like a punch to the gut.

"Do you know what he did to me?" Tears burn my eyes, forcing me to blink to keep them at bay. "No?" I ask as his jaw clenches without him offering up an answer. "For four years, he watched someone pretend to be my worst nightmare. Why?" I laugh when he remains silent. "Because this was always just a game to him. I was always a pawn."

"*Sí*," Julio says, but there's a flatness to his tone, neither confirming nor denying my statement. "But, though he sent me, I am not here for Mr. Villa. I'm here for you."

I bite my lip, unsure of whether or not to believe him. He could be lying, participating in another elaborate scheme.

But it's not like I have any other options.

"Chief Harrison has put an unofficial security detail on me," I blurt.

"*Sí*." He scowls, cutting his gaze to the doorway. "The bastards are especially…vigilant. Just getting to you was challenging."

"I don't trust him," I admit. "But I don't trust you, either. I can't trust anyone." I rip my hands through my hair, squeezing my eyes shut against the hopelessness building in my chest. "I can't—"

"I know," Julio says, his voice eerily level. "But I will confess that, while Mr. Villa sent me here, I came on my own. I wouldn't have otherwise," he adds. "But know that, for now, I am yours to command. Just say the word."

I frown. It's too tempting to consider. A trap?

Or a reprieve?

I only have a split second to decide. So I close my eyes and whisper, "Get me out of here."

"As you wish." His hand brushes mine, tugging me forward. I open my eyes as he drapes his coat over my shoulders and pulls the hood over my head. "Stay close."

Sixteen

ulio could be lying to me—but there is no mistaking his skill. When we exit the hospital minutes later without arousing suspicion, I have a clear idea of why Damien keeps him so close.

"How do I know you aren't planning to hand-deliver me to him?" I ask as the man ushers me into the back seat of a black car. But it's different from the model I'm used to. Key differences stick out: the tinted windows and smaller blueprint. Not one of Damien's.

"I could be," Julio says as he climbs into the driver's seat. "But I think you and I both know that Mr. Villa is a bit more…direct than this method."

He has a point.

"Chief Harrison says my father was poisoned by oleander," I say. "Do you think D-Damien… Could he have done it?"

"Never," Julio says without a shred of hesitation. "If Mr. Villa were to kill someone, there would be no question that he was the culprit. None. If anything, he would have to call me in to clean up the mess."

I have to consciously keep my mouth from dropping open. "You make it seem like he's done as much before."

He doesn't answer, staring resolutely through the windshield instead. His silence conveys more than any words could, however. A quiet reinforcement of his earlier warning: *The other Mr. Villa. He is a man you have not met, and you do not want to.*

"Where are you taking me?" I ask.

"Someplace safe. Neither Chief Harrison nor Mr. Villa will be able to find you, unless you desire to be found."

It sounds too good to be true. A mythical concept so beyond my current circumstances. I'm skeptical when Julio navigates us through a district in the heart of the city, finally stopping in front of a nondescript brownstone townhouse.

"If you make a list of your things, I can procure them for you," he explains while exiting the car and circling to my end. As he opens the door, he adds, "In the meantime, make yourself comfortable."

A suggestion made all too easy by the home's simple-but-clean layout. It's a step back from the luxury of Damien's suite, but a welcome change all things considered. The small living room contains just a modest array of brown leather furniture centered around a TV.

"I wonder if it's made the news?" I find myself blurting.

Julio quickly grabs a remote from an end table and flips the television on.

Sure enough, the blazing headline sports a grim update as to my father's status, but the main footage features a vaguely familiar man standing in front of a podium instead of a shot of the hospital. It must have been filmed hours earlier, because the sun is shining behind him, casting an aura of authority my father could have only dreamed of staging for himself.

Leaning toward the screen, I struggle to catch the words of his speech.

"…honored to have the family's blessing to continue on in my campaign," he says, his lips contorted in a charming grin. "I hope to make Heyworth and the rest of the Thornes proud. I do not accept this lightly."

"Our blessing?" As I speak, my thoughts clear and I'm finally able to put a name to the face. *Kyle Harrison.*

"The chief's son," Julio says with a familiarity that makes me suspect he's delved into the man's background more than I can imagine. "Political aspirations have shaped that boy since his days in prep school. Judging from your expression, I doubt your family has thrown their weight behind his endorsement, however."

"No," I croak. "I never gave him an answer."

"It seems they took that as confirmation," he says as the news coverage cuts back to the anchors seated in a newsroom. "Should I look into it?"

"Yes," I say without thinking through the consequences—such as potentially involving Damien even further into my life. "Something feels…wrong."

"*Sí*." He nods. "I'm on it."

He heads for the door, but I follow him.

"One other thing?"

"*¿Sí?*"

"Damien… Did he ever look into my case, truly? Or was it all just a lie?" My brain jumps to a terrifying conclusion before I can help it. "What if he knew Simon's true identity all along? Birds of a feather…"

"I admit that I am not sure," Julio says. "If he was involved, he did not utilize my skills."

"And if I wanted to confront him?" I ask, jutting my chin into the air. "Would you take me there?"

He frowns, seeming to mull it over. "Considering that I have pledged to be of use to you, it seems I wouldn't be able to refuse."

"Good." I start forward to the door. Paces away, I turn and sit on the couch instead. "Then keep him away from me. And keep me away from him."

*D*amien promised me that all of his resources would be at my disposal to aid in hunting down Simon's true identity. Now? I have only my phone, a paper towel serving as a makeshift notepad, and a pen sporting the logo of a hotel I found on the coffee table.

My scribbled notes are scattered—just pieces of information I subconsciously know I have no hope of piecing together on my own. Still, I force myself to put them into perspective.

Simon has been dead for four years according to my father.

Damien claimed he wasn't behind the continued presents, but someone else—someone powerful enough to hire skilled men every time to break into my apartment.

Men who scoured through my personal belongings and crept through my personal spaces. For years, leaving behind the ominous stench of cologne that I'd always linked to Simon…

And all along, Damien had watched.

"Don't get sidetracked," I scold myself. Drawing my knees up to my chin, I huddle against the back of the couch and continue to read, straining my eyes through the low light. The house is small, but I got some sleep in a small bedroom upstairs. When I awoke, I discovered an oversized shirt and pair of jeans Julio must have left for me, my makeshift detective uniform.

After tapping the pen on the paper, I start off with the easiest facts to comprehend: Chief Harrison claimed my father had been poisoned with oleander.

But Harrison's son is publicly claiming my father's endorsement.

Harrison also had access to my apartment.

But Harrison was also an acquaintance of my father's. I'm not sure if they were particularly close, but close enough that the man was a vague, though regular fixture at my father's events throughout the years. Could... Could he have been the one all those years ago to scribble my name onto a piece of paper that is now resting in Heyworth's security deposit box?

My temples throb, protesting the conflicting bits of information.

Then there's the matter of Lynn McKelvy. Her presents stopped when the real Simon died.

My tormentor didn't choose to continue haunting her. But why?

I'm making myself dizzy, pouring over the possibilities until my eyes burn—but reading is the only distraction I have from the low, rumbling noise gnawing at the edge of my awareness.

It's darker now. A blueish glow taints the room despite it being early in the afternoon. As I look up, a flash of white illuminates everything for a split second. And I freeze—the perfect victim for the thunder barreling through the quiet a heartbeat later.

I jump up, slamming my hands over my ears. But it's no use. I hear him anyway, no less real than he was twenty years ago.

Come out, come out, Juliana.

I see him: a shadow, lunging from the corners of the room, chasing me. Hunting me. I scream and turn to run. Escape. Clumsy limps hinder me. I'm not quick enough to avoid the edge of the end table. The glass catches my calf, sending me sideways, and I land hard, biting my tongue. A booming crash doesn't belong in my forest memories— neither does the icy pain dripping through my veins, concentrated over my right arm. But I can't move.

I can't breathe.

I just wait for the inevitable.

And, like clockwork, he comes for me.

"Juliana!" Grasping fingers clench my wrist, trying to pull me upright. "Ms. Thorne? *Mierda!* You're bleeding..." I know that voice. I think. That person...

No. He's not really here.

I'm not here.

I'm there.

I'm *there.*

Alone. I'm always alone…

"Shhh." A man's voice drips into my ear as if to directly challenge the thought—but it's not Simon's. Not Julio's, either. "Easy, *dulce niña*. I've got you."

He pulls me upright—lifting me from the floor, I realize. As I blink, the forest disappears, and I'm back in Julio's safe house. Rain lashes at the windows, goaded by another roar of thunder so strong it rattles the walls.

I flinch, fighting to cover my ears or my eyes—anything. But someone stronger pins me tight, smoothing their hands through my hair.

"I've got you," he murmurs. "I'm going to put you down." Somehow, he manages to navigate to the couch and pivots to lower me onto it. "*Mierda!* I need to assess your arm. I think you're still bleeding, sweet girl."

Still? My eyes fixate over a swath of glittering objects scattered over the floor. They gleam, illuminated by another flash of lightning: jagged pieces of glass. Part of the coffee table is shattered. By me. Numb, I look down at my arm, unsurprised by the dark-red substance coating my skin from forearm to fingertip.

"It feels deep," Damien hisses, probing the edge of the wound with his finger. "We need to apply pressure. Here." He sheds his tailored coat and uses touch to wad the sleeve of it against the worst of the bleeding.

"Don't," I croak as he cinches my forearm in a single fist. "Let go of me. Don't touch me!"

"*¡Detener!* I'm not leaving you alone like this."

I've never heard his tone so deep. Iron.

"You're in shock," he adds a fraction softer. The fingers of his opposite hand find the inside of my wrist, pressing along the tendon. "Your pulse is weak. You feel so damn cold—"

"Like you care." I want to shrug him off, but I'm too tired. I lean back against the cushions of the couch, my eyelids fluttering. "You're a liar. So is Julio—"

"He cares for you more than you realize," Damien growls, sounding gruffer once more. His grip tightens and I hiss, feeling the faintest tendrils of pain. "I had to beg him to tell me where you were. Me. *Beg.*" He scoffs at the absurdity, and through my blurred vision, I see his mouth twist into a frown. "I was worried about you."

"Leave me alone." My eyes drift shut again, blocking out his face. But not the pain. It's centered in my chest rather than my arm, however. Pulsing. Pinching. Burning. "I'll call the police—"

"You're too weak to move," Damien snarls. He pulls me in closer as if to prove it.

I can't fight him off. His heat is a vise, encasing me from all sides, squeezing out the numbing chill. This close to him, I feel everything. His hammering heartbeat radiating through his chest. His rapid breaths betraying how quickly he raced to me. His fear, pungent in the scent of his sweat.

My thoughts splinter, becoming too sharp. Too much.

"Let me go—"

"I never beg," he says into my ear, returning to that confession. "Never. I never pace my fucking suite in a frenzy. *¡Maldito sea!* I've never torn through the city like a madman looking for a woman who hides from me. I've never threatened to kill Julio with my bare fucking hands if he didn't reveal where she was. I wouldn't harm him," he says, almost as if to reassure himself of that fact. "But I still said it. Maybe in that moment, both of us believed it." His grip tightens even as he maintains the pressure on my injured arm. His breath scalds the side of my throat, his voice a low, insistent hum I can't ignore even if I wanted to. "I threatened him, *dulce niña*. All I could think about was you in this storm. A part of me hoped I'd find you standing here with a knife, ready to ward me off with violence. Unaffected. I would have left if I found you so."

Not panicked. And terrified. And weak.

"But you are only human," he tells me, his voice hoarse. "Human, and strong, and few could survive what you have. I forget that sometimes… The strength it takes. A weaker person—a weaker man—might turn off all emotion after such a betrayal. He might become bitter, and cold, and able to order murder in the same breath as he might order a meal. But you…" His lips nudge my skin, keeping me tethered despite another slamming roll of thunder. "You still love Heyworth Thorne, even after all he's done to you. You're strong enough to hold a vigil over his sickbed and defend him in public. You still fight to see the good. You believe in him, even as he hurt you."

"*You* hurt me," I rasp into his shoulder, too exhausted to pull away. "My father...he loves me. You don't—"

"Do you know when I realized, sweet girl? That I was a fool?" His voice relentlessly overpowers mine until I finally trail off. "It was when I found you in the woods. Even in your voice, I could hear it. Shock that I came for you. Gratitude. In that moment, all you wanted was someone. Me. You wanted me there. Not because of money or the many things you could extort. You were alone and you *needed* me. *Sí*, sweet girl. Such an innocent little request, and it shattered me to my goddamn core."

He nuzzles my shoulder, hesitating as I stiffen.

"I was wrong," he continues. "I was a bastard. Selfish. I don't deserve to be near you, let alone touch you like this." He slides his hand up and down my lower back anyway, gripping his fingers against the shape of me. "So you can feel no guilt or shame for using me. I'm here. Use me as your barrier against the storm. I can suffer that for you. When it's over, you will hate me again. You hate me still. I know... But I will stay anyway. I will comfort you anyway. I'll shoulder the burden so that you can protect your heart, sweet girl. Mine is already forfeit..."

I stiffen and peel my eyes open to an unfamiliar bed in an unfamiliar room. The simplistic color scheme recalls the memory of Julio's safe house. Sure enough, the view from the nearest window looks out on the same view of the residential area of the city. Safe. Quiet.

Far from the realm of my father or Damien—at least in theory.

I may be alone now, but another person left clues of their presence scattered around me, impossible to ignore. Like the blankets drawn carefully over me. As I kick them aside, I'm faced with the fact that someone removed my socks and shirt, making it easier for them—or a doctor—to access my right forearm. A crisp white bandage covers stitches, I assume. Vague images of watching someone maneuver a needle through my rent flesh reinforces that suspicion.

Someone also left a cup of coffee on the nightstand, now cold, as well as my abandoned cell phone—which could serve as a tracking device should they decide to utilize it. I grab it, intending to smash it, only to read the smattering of text messages flashing across the screen.

Diane: Stable condition. Doctors expect full recovery.

Sighing, I fall back against a mound of pillows. I should be relieved, full of naïve hopes of reconciliation and my father's health restored.

But I'm not.

Damien's words are in my head. *You love him. You forgive. Your strength.*

Love. All this time, I considered Simon's motives as hate. Hate for me. Sadistic glee at watching me suffer. A joy at causing pain—and maybe those emotions *had* driven his initial attack.

But his replacement? What would drive a man to torment a woman for years? In a way, Damien has never shied away from his reasoning: the love that he claimed kept me from becoming someone like him. Love for his brother that drove him to despise my father. Love that became pain.

And maybe the true imposter-Simon had the same motivations guiding him? Love for someone, the way my father loves me.

The theory haunts me as I climb off the mattress only to find a pair of clothing folded neatly at the foot of the bed. Reluctantly, I change into the clean sweater and pants, and then I find a bathroom down the hall to wash up in.

I look awful. A haunted shadow of the beautiful Juliana Thorne I spent years striving to be. Anything to make Heyworth Thorne proud. Anything to prove that I was worth living the life that should have been Leslie's.

Anything to hide from the trauma no one else could see.

My phone is in my grip, I realize as I return to the hall. Damien could be using it already, listening in on my indecision. Tracking my every move.

I bring the device to my ear, but it doesn't ring. I have to dial the number myself and wait for an answer from the other end.

"Juliana…" Damien sounds wary this morning. A raw note of exhaustion betrays his lack of sleep.

How long did he linger after having his private doctor stitch me up? How long did he lie in bed beside me to the point where I could still smell him when I woke up? How long has he kept his own phone close, hoping I'd call? Knowing I would?

"I can have the police there in minutes if you would like to report my actions as assault."

There's no mocking humor tainting his accent. I can't tell if he's serious or taunting. Maybe that's the point. Dealing with him is a game, pushing my heart to its limits. Knowing at any second he might caress it with the tip of a paintbrush or stab a blade through it.

"I think I know who's behind the attacks," I admit. "I think he's going to try killing my father again. Then…I think he's going to kill me."

"*¿Sí?*" A fierceness makes him sound more intimidating than ever.

"It could be you," I admit. "The one killing everyone involved in your brother's case. The real culprit behind the attack on me. You really were behind the Simon imposter. This is all your game…"

"*Sí,*" he admits. "It could be me. I won't insult your intelligence by proclaiming my innocence. You have no reason to believe me."

But he's wrong. And that's the terrifying part.

"It could be Mateo," I add. "He's angry. No one would believe he wasn't capable."

"*Sí,*" Damien admits. "Even I, at times, am not sure of what he's capable of."

"But I don't think he is. He's too angry. Too driven by rage. He would be sloppy."

But this killer is clean. Precise. His goal isn't to sow pain and fear—it's more calculated than that. In his view, maybe even pure.

"I think you can help me draw the real killer out into the open," I say cautiously. "But you'd risk exposing yourself and sending your empire crashing down around you. You'd have to risk lowering your precious mask and letting the world see the monster underneath. And you'd have to do so knowing that, even then, I still can't forgive you."

His silence ratchets the tension building in my chest, squeezing every ounce of blood from my heart. I'm dizzy, swaying in time with my surging pulse.

"Could you?" I croak, finally demanding an answer.

"Tell me what you need," he says. "Tell me. And I will do it."

SEVENTEEN

After I hang up with Damien and venture downstairs, I find Julio waiting for me in the living room. He stands near the now missing coffee table, sweeping what seems to be small shards of glass into a dustpan. As I approach, he sets his broom aside and faces me, swiping his hands over the front of his professional suit.

"Morning, Ms. Thorne."

"Thank you," I say, forcing the words past my thickened throat. "I'm sorry if I caused any trouble between you and your employer."

"*No hay problema.*" He waves me off and returns to his broom. "I'll clean up this mess and I have Mr. Villa's permission to move you to another location. One that he does not know of and will never discover without your permission."

I don't even need to see his face to know it's the truth.

"Why would you do this for me?"

"In some ways, it's selfish, Ms. Thorne," he admits, meeting my gaze directly. "I'm doing this for him. We had our bargain, after all."

Make Damien earn my forgiveness—not if but *when* he hurts me.

"I need a favor," I say, changing the subject.

"*¿Sí?*" Instantly, he stands to his full height, crossing his hands over his front. "Say the word."

"I can explain on the way there." I head to the door. "The first favor, though, may test your skills…"

"Oh?" He follows, raising an eyebrow. "How so, if I may ask?"

I look him over, biting my lower lip. "Well, I'll need you to pretend to be my publicist, for one."

Standing in front of a sea of reporters, I can't escape an overwhelming sense of irony. It's the world my father cherished. The world I thought he'd forsaken me for. A world of glitz, and glamor, and deception.

Despite being hastily compiled, my "news conference" has attracted enough reporters to ensure broadcast coverage—yet, in some ways, I feel no different than I did lying naked in front of a theater of strangers at Damien's discretion.

On display, yet…

In control.

"Good morning," I say, speaking into a microphone affixed to a small podium. The ballroom of the Lariat looms behind me, a perfect gilded backdrop. "My father and I would like to thank the well-wishers and those who have kept us in your prayers during this difficult time. I admit that, in the chaos, my family has been quiet, and I thank the media for respecting our privacy. However…" I clear my throat as doubt creeps in.

I could be wrong. With Daddy's life on the line, I could be placing him in more danger. I could be gambling everything with nothing at all to gain.

"After much reflection, my father and I have decided that we welcome all inquiry into the Borgetta case. There was evidence that admittedly wasn't allowed to be presented to the jury. Other suspects that deserve to be questioned. This terrible ordeal has helped my family to realize that Mathias Villa also deserves justice, no matter where its harsh light may shine. In that event, on behalf of my father, I suspend his campaign for mayor—as well as withdraw any endorsements that may have been granted on our behalf."

An audible gasp rises from the crowd.

"My father's record may not be perfect," I add, forcing myself to keep going. "We thought he was a hero, but he is only human. Therefore, I'm calling for an inquiry into all his past cases, extending to his time as a defense attorney. I think it was his intention before his health failed. The truth must come out into the open, no matter who it may touch. My father may be human, but some men become monsters. Thank you."

I turn away as the throng of reporters erupts, issuing a barrage of questions. It should be harder than it is to ignore them. Luckily, Julio serves as an effective barrier, falling into step behind me as I escape via the residential wing and enter my suite.

"I'll be out front, Ms. Thorne," he warns before retreating to his chosen end of the hall.

I enter my suite and shrug my coat off, tossing it aside. Sighing, I move to the couch, observing the view. From here Damien's painting is a chilling distraction from even the breathtaking landscape of the city stretched beyond it. The woman eyes me warily, her empty gaze a warning. *This is what he could do to you.*

Hollow.

But wait… Her irises are darker, swollen, her lips bitten red. Long, dark hair cascades down her shoulders as she writhes upon a bed of tiny white flowers. Oleander.

The painter exposed her entire body in microscopic focus. Her breasts. Her hips. The jagged scar along her thigh. Vulnerability exudes from her, matching the rigid posture of his previous muses. But there's a strength to this woman that sets her apart. A stubborn tilt to her chin. A sternness in her mouth. The artist tried desperately to capture as much of her soul as he could—but it was only a fraction. She holds on to her secrets, daring him to capture what little he could. Daring him to crave more.

It's so beautiful. So raw…

I don't realize I'm not alone until it's too late. Footsteps rush toward me as pain rips through my throat—the result of a hand clenching tight from behind.

"You little bitch." Chief Harrison sounds more amused than angry—but fury leeches into his fingertips. They dig into my skin so hard that the world goes black for a second. Gurgling noises die in my throat as I claw at his grip. I succeed in loosening it only a fraction, peeling one of his fingers from my windpipe. "How long have you known?" he wonders, eerily calm even as I resist. "How much did that spineless little bastard tell you?"

His grip loosens enough for me to croak, "My father?"

He laughs. "How did he spin it?" he wonders, shoving me forward, toward the glass doors leading to my balcony. "Him, the wonderful, doting father. You, the naïve innocent he had to protect from herself. When, in reality, he was a fucking coward."

"You told him about me," I say hoarsely. "You gave him my name—"

"I gave him a chance at redemption." He tightens his grip, drawing tears from my eyes. "A chance to bring a monster to justice. The man who killed your little friend… Heyworth represented him. Took his money and then helped him walk. And he went right across state lines and did it again."

"So you gave Thorne my name," I say, standing on tiptoe—the only position that loosens the pressure on my throat enough to breathe. "Why?"

"So he could find the abandoned little victim," Harrison says coldly. "Pump her damaged brain for information. Feed her what she needed to know, enough to form convincing testimony. Then get her into a foster home where the parents could be easily 'convinced' to force her to testify. If they lived in my jurisdiction, I could claim credit for the collar, and Thorne would have his guilty conscience wiped clean."

I picture the plan as he relays it. That traumatized little girl would have been easily manipulated. But forced to face Simon again, she would have shattered.

"He was too soft," Harrison hisses, following the same thread of logic. "Too weak."

"He adopted me instead," I surmise. "As my guardian, he refused to let me testify without hard evidence."

And in some ways, he's sheltered me ever since. Justice demanded a cruel solution, but he was too selfish. Not out of pride, but because he loved me too much.

"The prick was terrified of Thorne," Harrison says with a chilling laugh. "He taunted his other victims, but never you. Not the precious Juliana. *You* were his special one—"

"Who was he?" I wince as his grip tightens.

"Who?" He laughs again, which raises goosebumps over my skin. "You really are that naïve? Think carefully. Your father whored himself in front of any donor with money, but there was *one* in particular he never paraded you around. Do you remember?"

No... Not at first. Then, suddenly, a name comes to mind like a light flipping on.

"Gerald Wellington," I say hoarsely.

"Yes." Harrison nods. "A sociopathic degenerate with too much money and time on his hands. Rumor has it that he liked to test the innocent. Play little games. Like cornering two weak little girls, perhaps? Then making one of them choose who got to die."

The world transforms for a split second. I'm there again, trapped in the woods, running for my life. Running from Simon.

"Thorne knew who the bastard was from day one," Harrison says, chuckling at the irony. "He made sure Wellington knew as much too. Thorne ensured the man was all but a recluse, but he still played with his victims. He couldn't resist. The ones who weren't you at least."

Like Lynn McKelvy.

"So you reminded me for him," I rasp, horrified. "It was you. All this time, it was you."

The police department supplied my father's security, even during the time he was mayor, giving him unfettered access. To my room. My homes. My life.

"A little reminder in case Thorne ever changed his mind." He laughs, grinding his grip into my windpipe but not hard enough to obscure it entirely. "He may have forgotten, but you never would, Daddy's little princess."

"And the Borgetta murder?" I choke out. "You made my father suppress the evidence that could have acquitted Mathias Villa. Why?"

"Thorne told you that?" He shoves me forward and reaches out with his free hand, unlocking the sliding glass door. Cool air blows the hair from my face and I instinctively stiffen, resisting his grip even though it's futile. I have no chance in hell of overpowering him. "I should pay him another little visit—"

"Kyle killed her, didn't he?" I say in a rush, hoping to keep his attention on this topic. "His name was among the list of suspects. Suspects you refused to have questioned in full. He killed her—"

"Shut up!" He wrenches me around, using his size as leverage to drag me out onto the balcony.

I reach out blindly, grasping the railing before I can fall over the edge.

"I think it was your precious Damien Villa," he declares. "Murdering the key players. Killing your father with oleander. Causing your suicide. In fact, I'll make sure there's enough damage to your skull to obscure the bruising on your throat." He tugs me closer to the railing. Below, my coveted view looms, desolate this time of the morning.

"But it's too late. My father kept the evidence," I say. "I've already had it sent to the news—"

"Hearsay," Harrison says. He lets me go, his lips quirked, his smile chilling. "We both know that, as your father feared, nothing sticks without fucking evidence. So I suggest you jump on your own. It will be more conclusive that way."

"Evidence," I rasp, cradling my throat. "Like a voice recording? Of you confessing like some cartoon villain."

His smug expression slips, his eyebrow raising. "What?"

I nod to the interior of my suite. "You're smart. You've monitored me undetected for over twenty years. But someone else took up your game. He's played it better. My apartment's been bugged for four years. He's captured everything. Every gift. Every henchman you've had break into my suite."

"Villa?" He scoffs. "The bastard isn't untouchable. You think you matter to him? I have enough dirt to bury him *and* his fucking empire. No. I think he'll sit back and watch you die."

And maybe he's right. Maybe this was all another layer of a twisted, sick game?

Damien will get his revenge threefold and no one would ever be the wiser.

I almost believe it…

Until I hear him.

"I don't believe that will be the case, chief." His accent rides the gathering wind, more cutting than ever.

I turn, my heart stopping at the sight of him looming over the threshold of the balcony.

His hands are outstretched on either side of him, a subtle clue that he navigated here without his cane. "Step aside. Your men should be arriving any minute to take you into custody."

Chief Harrison chokes on a sound between a laugh and a growl. "Are you playing the hero now, Villa?" he wonders. His eyes cut to me, his smile dastardly smug. "Did you tell her? How you advertised her little show to the members of your club?"

My thoughts slow, my heart clenching like a fist over any blood flow.

"Oh yes," he murmurs, eyeing me lewdly up and down. "The bastard told everyone who you were. Fucking yourself like a whore—"

"Lies," Damien says simply. "You know I would never betray your trust. Never."

Even though he lied to me. Even though he let a monster creep into my life every single year for so damn long.

"It was quite the show," Harrison says, inching forward a step. "I'll be sure to leak it to the press. I'm sure that's what he wanted. They all know, you little bitch. And if you think this blind bastard can save you…"

He lunges, his hands reaching for my throat.

But they never make contact. A horrible gurgling noise mingles with a crack sharper than any I've heard as Chief Harrison's head jerks. The angle is too odd. Unnatural. His eyes stare blankly ahead, his body slumping…

As if from far away, I hear my own high-pitched whisper, "Oh my god—"

"Breathe," Damien snaps. It's his hands releasing Harrison's throat. His body that captures the massive officer as though he weighs nothing. Even without his sight, he pivots, navigating his way into my living room, the body in tow.

A chill renders me numb as I remember his confession from all those nights ago. *I worked hard to change the man I was.*

A man who moves with a predatory grace as he dumps a dead body beside my coffee table and prods the black device sticking from his ear. "Julio." He says a stream of Spanish. Then he breaks off and turns to me. "Juliana." His soft tone triggers the tears trapped behind my eyes until now.

I blink and they fall, painting my cheeks.

"Sweet, *dulce niña*." He takes a step forward and then hesitates. "I'll take all responsibility," he says. "I will turn myself in to the police. I will reveal my part in Harrison's deception. If that is what you want, I will do it now. Julio is with the police… I will."

He should be lying. It should be so easy to doubt him now. God, I want to. I need to.

"The bastard was lying," he adds, cupping his ear again, ready to dish out another series of commands. "I would never reveal you to them. Never—"

"He was there," I croak, finally placing the odd smell I sensed in the air. Cigar smoke. *Harrison,* lingering somewhere in the atrium during my exhibition. Damien even warned me himself: The chief knew to keep quiet about the club. Perhaps because he was a member all along. "He knew about my scar." And now his pointed mentioning of it makes sense. "He guessed…"

Relief visibly robs Damien's body of tension. Only belatedly does he seem to remember his promise. "Julio," he murmurs into his headset. "Send up the police. Tell them—"

"No." I don't even know where the refusal comes from. It's wrong, going against everything my father taught me about justice. But if I've learned anything at all from recent events, it's that sometimes heroes are the worst kinds of monsters. And sometimes their victims are inherently selfish. Could my father survive his ordeal and then outlast a murder trial with his decades-old secrets at the heart of it? No. "I…I want him to disappear."

"Are you sure?" His posture changes in the blink of an eye.

I'm too exhausted to nod or give some kind of nonverbal agreement. I have to say it. "Yes."

He nods and prods his headset. "Julio. Tell the police Harrison has escaped the suite. Possibly through a back stairwell. Ensure the cameras malfunction and then make the arrangements. You know the ones." He turns back to me, his head cocked, picking up my rapid breathing. "Did he hurt you?"

I can't lie. I can't seem to speak anymore, either. I stand, moisture rolling down my face, my body swaying.

"*Mierda.*" He crosses to me, capturing me in his arms before I can fall. "Stay with me, sweet girl." He runs his fingers along my shoulder, inching toward my throat. When his thumb nudges my throbbing windpipe, I wince. "The flesh is inflamed. You're wheezing," he deduces, drawing his hand away. In response, his grip around me only tightens, drawing me into his chest. "If he did lasting damage, I'll resurrect the bastard just to kill him again—"

"Stop," I rasp, too limp to physically fight him off. "Just…"

"I know, sweet girl," he murmurs, bringing his mouth against the crook of my shoulder. "I've frightened you. But I'm not leaving. Not now. Not until I know you're safe."

With him? A man who killed someone in front of me? A man who smells like sin and perfection despite the persistent stench of Harrison's cigar scent permeating the air? A man who tightens his grip even further when my knees buckle and I'm in danger of falling once again?

"Easy." He guides me back and eases me onto the couch. "This is a dream," he tells me, his voice taking on a polished calm. It's colder. Harder. Broken. "I will handle everything. Just sleep, sweet girl. Sleep."

Sunlight streams in through my bedroom window, painting the muted color scheme in a golden glow. It's as if nature itself decided to conspire with the whims of Damien Villa. He told me to forget—but I remember resolutely.

For now, the dark, grisly images are mere snippets, but they linger in my mind as I stagger into my living room. Unsurprisingly, reality contradicts nearly every single one.

There is no dead police chief lying on my carpet. The sliding glass door to my balcony is closed. Every item and piece of furniture is perfectly in place. When I scan the top news stories on my cell phone, only my father's improving status makes the headlines. The only flaw in the design I notice is when I pass the fridge and spot my distorted reflection.

Gasping, I brush my fingers along my throat. The violent, purplish discoloration could be a trick of the light—but the agony I've been ignoring with every breath I take isn't.

A part of me giggles internally as I slump against the counter, my face in my hands. New memories to torment me. A new monster to haunt my nightmares. I brace my hands over the marble in front of me, and by accident, the fingers of my left brush something unfamiliar: a folded piece of paper.

On it, someone scribbled: *Julio is stationed on you twenty-four-seven unless you decide to revoke him. I've taken the liberty of removing your garbage and it has been disposed of. I'll set up meetings with any remaining mutual acquaintances. If you need me, you know where to find me, dulce niña. Otherwise, I will respect whatever boundary you set. Adios, Damien.*

EIGHTEEN

Some claimed that the bigger a man was the harder he fell.

But sometimes he needed to fall. Only then, in the aftermath of the chaos, could he reassemble from the broken pieces the parts of himself that had been lost in the façade. He wasn't perfect. He wasn't a monolith of wisdom, integrity, or stellar judgment.

He was human.

And it took my father nearly a grueling month of intensive recovery to realize that. His smile isn't smug as he faces a throng of reporters waiting beyond the hospital's main doors. He looks tired and older than ever.

But in his exhausted, haggard expression, I see hints of the man who rescued me all those years ago. My old childhood hero.

"Should we face the cavalry?" he wonders as Diane and I flank him on either side, each of us holding a papery hand of his. His security team surrounds us at a respectful distance, but as we step from the shelter of the building, they provide no cover from the avalanche of questions.

"Mr. Thorne! Do you regret withdrawing from public office?"

"Is it true that you plan to publicly renounce your judgment in the Borgetta murder case?"

"Ms. Thorne! Are you still involved with Damien Villa?"

As we finally climb into the waiting limo, the metal frame mutes the noise enough for me to hear my father ask, "You're still coming to dinner, sweet pea?"

"Yes," I rasp. "I just have something to take care of. That's all."

Something that requires that the driver drops me off at the private residential entrance of the Lariat. Leaning toward him, I kiss my father on the cheek. "I'll see you later tonight."

Questions burn in his gaze even as he physically bites them back. "Of course, sweet pea."

I enter the hotel and cross the lobby. My hand slips into the pocket of my coat, withdrawing a slip of paper I'd crumpled and thrown away—only to salvage later—so many times that the font has worn away in places. An invitation to a private gallery held in a more secluded ballroom of the Lariat.

A part of me knows better than to attend. I should have been packing my things, preparing to move in with my parents at their newly purchased family compound on the outskirts of the city. I should have been helping my father prepare his public address on his role in the injustice against Mathias Villa.

Anything but inching down a deserted hallway and entering a closed room.

This showing lacks the pomp and grandeur of Sampson's first splashy outing. Only a few paintings are on display: each one portraying the same woman in excruciating detail.

I move, drawn forward to a painting hanging at the back of the space. It's beautiful, even if grotesquely raw in a way. Pale limbs were on shameless display. Scars. Curves. Pimples.

But her eyes are the most striking—almost impossibly so. Tears brim in them. And anger. And rage. A pain so raw that it takes my breath away.

"My finest work, I think," a man announces, his voice low near my ear. "What are your thoughts?"

My breath catches, and I reach out, unconcerned as my fingers brush the canvas directly. Whirls and divots in the layers of paint reveal a painstaking level of artistry. Devotion to capturing every single strand of hair. Every flaw that could be discerned through touch.

Everything about *me* in stroke after stroke.

"I'm afraid that you keep straining the theory that you are truly blind, Mr. Villa," I rasp.

"Not blind…" Fingers like silk caress the flesh of my shoulder bared by the neckline of my sweater. I flinch, but something won't let me pull away. "No man could risk being so vulnerable around you. He must employ all of his senses, *sí*—an arsenal of senses to decipher you. Smell. Touch. Taste."

I shiver as his breath warms the back of my throat, creeping like wildfire.

"I'm sure even this painting portrays only a fraction."

"I shouldn't be here," I admit, blinking. "I should be…"

Furious. Hateful. Bitter.

"I know," he says. "You have no reason to forgive me, and I don't have the right to demand it."

"So why all this?" I gesture to the surrounding space. To the other paintings hanging just beyond my line of sight. "I could still hate you."

"I know," he says. "You have every right to."

"Didn't you get what you wanted? My father is going to publicly renounce his own judgment. Your brother will be vindicated. Though I'm sure you've already gotten your revenge."

According to the news reports issued earlier this morning, Kyle Harrison has vanished from his expensive penthouse home, presumably on the run given new evidence brought to light. I know the truth, however, and Damien grits his teeth, confirming it.

"So why contact me?" I ask.

"Stupidity. Insanity, perhaps," he says. "For a man with my resources, I'm not used to begging for what I want."

My heart lurches, ramming against my rib cage. "And what do you want?"

"To start over," he says simply. "I want to introduce myself to the beautiful woman who visited my exhibition and expressed interest in my work like no one else. I want her to know that I am willing to earn her trust through any means available to me. I want her to know…"

"What?" I croak when he falls silent.

"I want her to know that I will never abandon her. Whether she can forgive me or not."

Tears spill from my eyes, painting my cheeks. "I'm hungry," I blurt.

Another deliberate step brings him closer still. "Oh?"

"Yes. I'm in the mood for pizza." Turning on my heel, I move for the hall, calling back, "You have five minutes before I change my mind."

His laugh brings fluttering butterflies to life in my stomach. "As you wish, Ms. Thorne. I am yours to command."

Hey there!

Thank you so much for reading! If you enjoyed the story, please leave a review and recommend the book to any friend you think would love this twisted world. You'd have my eternal gratitude. Even a short sentence goes a long way!

Then, come join the rest of us dark romance lovers in my Facebook Group where you can get snippets, sneak peeks of upcoming books and even help vote on aspects of future novels.

Come to the dark side:

https://www.facebook.com/groups/lanasbeautifulmonsters/

WANT MORE STUFF TO READ?

Join my newsletter and get a **free book**! Plus, you get to stay updated with any new releases, random giveaways and exclusive sneak peeks!

https://www.lanaskybooks.com/newsletter

Other Novels: https://lanaskybooks.com/

ABOUT THE
AUTHOR

Lana Sky is a reclusive writer in the United States who spends most of her time daydreaming about complex male characters and parenting her Cockapoo Joey. She writes dark, twisted romance across several genres. Her titles include everything from mafia romance to vampires.

facebook.com/AuthorLanaSky

twitter.com/lanasky101

amazon.com/author/lanasky

pinterest.com/lanasky101

goodreads.com/lanasky

instagram.com/lanasky101

bookbub.com/authors/lana-sky

For more titles by Lana Sky, please visit:

https://www.lanaskybooks.com

www.ingramcontent.com/pod-product-compliance
Lightning Source LLC
Chambersburg PA
CBHW071749190726
48292CB00003B/916